Horace Smith

Interludes, being two essays, a story and some verses

Horace Smith

Interludes, being two essays, a story and some verses

ISBN/EAN: 9783744749077

Printed in Europe, USA, Canada, Australia, Japan

Cover: Foto ©Andreas Hilbeck / pixelio.de

More available books at **www.hansebooks.com**

INTERLUDES

BEING

TWO ESSAYS, A STORY, AND

SOME VERSES

BY

HORACE SMITH

𝔏𝔬𝔫𝔡𝔬𝔫
MACMILLAN AND CO
AND NEW YORK
1892

CONTENTS.

A FARRAGO OF VERSES *(continued)*—

ESSAYS.

ESSAYS.

I. ON CRITICISM.

CRITICISM is the art of judging. As reasonable persons
we are called upon to be constantly pronouncing judgment, and either acting upon such judgment ourselves or
inviting others to do so. I do not know how anything
can be more important with respect to any matter than
the forming a right judgment about it. We pray that we
may have "a right judgment in all things." I am aware
that it is an old saying that "people are better than
their opinions," and it is a mercy that it is so, for very
many persons not only are full of false opinions upon
almost every subject, but even think that it is of no
consequence what opinions they hold. Whether a
particular action is morally right or wrong, or whether a
book or a picture is really good or bad, is a matter upon
which they form either no judgment or a wrong one with
perfect equanimity. The secret of this state of mind is,
I think, that it is on the whole too much bother to form
a correct judgment; and it is so much easier to let things
slide, and to take the good the gods provide you, than to
carefully hold the scales until the balance is steady. But

A

can anybody doubt that this abdication of the seat of
judgment by large numbers of people is most hurtful to
mankind? Does anyone believe that there would be so
many bad books, bad pictures, and bad buildings in the
world if people were more justly critical? Bad things
continue to be produced in profusion, and worse things
are born of them, because a vast number of people do not
know that the things are bad, and do not care, even if
they do know. What sells the endless trash published
every day? Not the *few* purchasers who buy what is
vile because they like it, but the *many* purchasers who
do not know that the things are bad, and when they are
told so, think there is not much harm in it after all.
In short, they think that judging rightly is of no consequence and only a bore.

But I think I shall carry you all with me when I say
that this society, almost by its very *raison d'être*, desires
to form just and proper judgments; and that one of the
principal objects which we have in view in meeting
together from time to time is to learn what should be
thought, and what ought to be known; and by com-
paring our own judgments of things with those of our
neighbours, to arrive at a just modification of our rough
and imperfect ideas.

Although criticism is the act of judging in general,
and although I shall not strictly limit my subject to any
particular branch of criticism, yet naturally I shall be
led to speak principally of that branch of which we—
probably all of us—think at once when the word is
mentioned, viz., literary and artistic criticism. I think
if criticism were juster and fairer persons criticized
would submit more readily to criticism. It is certain

that criticism is generally resented. We—none of us—
like to be told our faults.
"Tell Blackwood," said Sir Walter Scott, "that I am
one of the Black Hussars of Literature who neither give
nor take criticism." Tennyson resented any interference
with his muse by writing the now nearly forgotten line
about "Musty, crusty Christopher." Byron flew into a
rhapsodical passion and wrote *English Bards and Scotch
Reviewers*—

"Ode, Epic, Elegy, have at you all."

He says—

"A man must serve his time to every trade
Save censure. Critics all are ready made.
Take hackney'd jokes from Miller, got by rote,
With just enough of learning to misquote;
A mind well skilled to find or forge a fault;
A turn for punning—call it Attic salt;
To Jeffrey go, be silent and discreet,—
His pay is just ten sterling pounds per sheet;
Fear not to lie, 'twill seem a sharper hit;
Shrink not from blasphemy, 'twill pass for wit;
Care not for feeling—pass your proper jest,—
And stand a critic, hated yet caress'd."

Lowell retorted upon his enemies in the famous *Fable for
Critics*. Swift, in his *Battle of the Books*, revenges himself upon Criticism by describing her. "She dwelt on
the top of a snowy mountain in Nova Zembla. There
Momus found her extended in her den upon the spoils
of numberless volumes, half devoured. At her right
hand sat Ignorance, her father and husband, blind with
age; at her left Pride, her mother, dressing her up in
the scraps of paper herself had torn. About her played
her children Noise and Impudence, Dulness and

Vanity, Pedantry and Ill-manners. The goddess herself had claws like a cat. Her head, ears, and voice resembled those of an ass." Bulwer (Lord Lytton) flew out against his critics, and was well laughed at by Thackeray for his pains. Poets are known as the *genus irritabile*, and I do not know that prose writers, artists, or musicians are less susceptible. Most of us will remember Sheridan's *Critic*—

Sneer : " I think it wants incident."

Sir Fretful : "Good Heavens, you surprise me ! Wants incident ! I am only apprehensive that the incidents are too crowded."

Dangle : " If I might venture to suggest anything, it is that the interest rather falls off in the fifth act."

Sir Fretful : " Rises, I believe you mean, sir."

Mrs. Dangle : " I did not see a fault in any part of the play from the beginning to the end."

Sir Fretful : " Upon my soul the women are the best judges after all."

In short, no one objects to a favourable criticism, and almost every one objects to an unfavourable one. All men ought, no doubt, to be thankful for a just criticism ; but I am afraid they are not. As a result, to criticize is to be unpopular. Nevertheless, it is better to be unpopular than to be untruthful.

> " The truth once out,—and wherefore should we lie ?—
> The Queen of Midas slept, and so can I."

I am going to do a rather dreadful thing. I am going to divide criticism into six heads. By the bye, I am not sure that sermons now-a-days are any better than they used to be in the good old times, when there were always three heads at least to every sermon. Criticism should be—1. Appreciative. 2. Proportionate. 3. Appropriate. 4. Strong. 5. Natural. 6. *Bonâ fide.*

1. *Criticism should be appreciative.*

By this I mean, not that critics should always praise, but that they should understand. They should see the thing as it is and comprehend it. This is the rock upon which most criticisms fail—want of knowledge. In reading the lives of great men, how often are we struck with the want of appreciation of their fellows. Who admired Turner's pictures until Turner's death? Who praised Tennyson's poems until Tennyson was quite an old man? Nay, I am afraid some of us have laughed at those who endeavoured to ask our attention to what we called the daubs of the one or the doggerel of the other.[1] This, I think, should teach us not even to attempt to criticize until we are sure that we appreciate. Yet what a vast amount of criticism there is in the world which errs (like Dr. Johnson) from sheer ignorance. When Sir Lucius O'Trigger found fault with Mrs. Malaprop's language she naturally resented such ignorant criticism. "If there is one thing more than another upon which I pride myself, it is the use of my oracular tongue and a nice derangement of epitaphs." It was absurd to have one's English criticized by any Irishman. It is said that "it's a pity when lovely women talk of things that they don't understand"; but I am afraid that men are equally given to the same vice. I have

---

[1] Milton only received £10 for *Paradise Lost*, and there is a good story told that some one copied it out in manuscript and sent it successively to three great London publishers, who all declined it as unsuitable to the public taste.

heard men give the most confident opinions upon subjects which they don't in the least understand, which
nobody expects them to understand, nor have they had
any opportunity for acquiring the requisite knowledge.
But I suppose an Englishman is nothing if he is not
dictatorial, and has a right to say that the pictures in
the Louvre are "orrid" or that the Colosseum is a
"himposition." "I don't know what they mean by
Lucerne being the Queen of the Lakes," said a Yankee
to me, "but I calc'late Lake St. George is a doocid deal
bigger." The criticism was true as far as it went, but
the man had no conception of beauty.

> "Each might his several province well command
> Would all but stoop to what they understand."

The receipt given for an essay on Chinese Metaphysics
was, look out China under the letter C and metaphysics
under the letter M, and combine your information.
"Would you mind telling me, sir, if the Cambridge boat
keeps time or not to-day?" said a man on the banks of
the Thames to me. He explained that he was a political-
meeting reporter on the staff of a penny paper, and the
sporting reporter was ill. Sometimes the want of
appreciation appears in a somewhat remarkable manner, as where a really good performance is praised for
its blemishes and not for its merits. This may be done
from a desire to appear singular or from ignorance.
The popular estimate is generally wrong from want of
appreciation. The majority of people praise what is not
worthy of praise and dislike what is. So that it is almost
a test of worthlessness that the multitudes approve.
Baron Bramwell, in discharging a prisoner at the Old

Bailey, made what he thought some appropriate obser-
vations, which were followed by a storm of applause in
the crowded court. The learned judge, with that caustic
humour which distinguishes him, looked up and said,
" Bless me ! I'm afraid I must have said something very
foolish." An amusing scene occurred outside a barrister's lodgings during the Northampton Assizes. Two
painters decorating the exterior of the lodgings were
overheard as follows :—"Seen the judge, Bill?" "Ah,
I see him. Cheery old swine !" "See the sheriff too?"
"Yes, I see him too. I reckon he got that place through
interest. Been to church; they tell me the judge
preached 'em a long sarmon. Pomp and 'umbug I call
that !" This was no doubt genuine criticism, but it was
without knowledge. These men were probably voters for
Bradlaugh, and the judge and the sheriff were to them
the embodiment of a hateful aristocracy. These painters
little knew how much the judge would like to be let off
even listening to the sermon, and how the sheriff had
resorted to every dodge to escape from his onerous and
thankless office.

It is recorded in the Life of Lord Houghton that
Prince Leopold, being recommended to read Plutarch
for Grecian lore, got the British Plutarch by mistake,
and laid down the Life of Sir Christopher Wren in great
indignation, exclaiming there was hardly anything about
Greece in it.

I am sure, too, that in order to understand the work
of another we must have something more than knowledge ; we must have some sympathy with the work. I
do not mean that we must necessarily praise the exe-
cution of it; but we must be in such a frame of mind

that the success of the work would give us pleasure. I am sure someone says somewhere that à man whose first emotion upon seeing anything good is to undervalue it will never do anything good of his own. It argues a want of genius in ourselves if we fail to see.it in others; unless, indeed, we do really see it, and only *say* we don't out of envy. This is very shameful. I had rather do like some amiable people I have known, disparage the work of a friend in order to set others praising it.

Criticism should therefore be appreciative in two ways. The critic should bring the requisite amount and kind of knowledge and the proper frame of mind and temper.

2. *Criticism should be proportionate.*

By this I mean that the language in which we speak of anything should be proportioned to the thing spoken of. If you speak of St. Paul's Church, Beckenham, as vast, grand, magnificent, you have no language left wherewith to describe St. Paul's, London. If you call Millais' Huguenots sublime or divine, what becomes of the Madonná St. Sisto of Raphael? If you describe Longfellow's poetry as the feeblest possible trash, the coarsest and most unparliamentary language could alone express your contempt of Martin Tupper.

" What's the good of calling a woman a Wenus, Samivel ? " asked the elder Weller. What indeed ! The elder Weller probably perceived that the language would be out of all proportion to the object of Samivel's affections. Of course, something may be allowed to a generous enthusiasm, and, with regard to this fault in criticism, it should perhaps be said that exaggerated

praise is not so base in its beginning or so harmful in
the end as exaggerated blame. From the use of the
former Dr. Johnson defended himself with his usual
vigour. Boswell presumed to find fault with him for
saying that the death of Garrick had eclipsed the gaiety
of nations. Johnson : "I could not have said more,
nor less. It is the truth. His death did eclipse, it was
like a storm." Boswell : "But why nations? Did his
gaiety extend further than his own nation?" Johnson :
"Why, sir, some exaggeration must be allowed. Besides,
'nations' may be said—if we allow the Scotch to be a
nation, and to have gaiety,—which they have not."

But there is more in this matter of proportion than at
first meets the eye. How often do we converse with a
man whose language we wonder at and cannot quite
make out. It is somehow unsatisfactory. We do not
quite like it, yet there is nothing particular to dislike.
Suddenly we perceive that there is a want of perspective,
or perhaps a want of what artists call value. His
mountains are mole-hills, and his mole-hills are mountains. His colouring is so badly managed that the effect
of distance, light, and shade are lost. Thus a man will
so insist upon the use of difficult words by George Elliot
that a person unacquainted with her writings would think
that the whole merit or demerit of that author lay in her
vocabulary. A man will so exalt the pathos of Dickens
or Thackeray that he will throw their wit and humour
into the background. Some person's only remark on
seeing Turner's Modern Italy will be that the colours are
cracked, or, upon reading Sterne, that he always wrote
"you was" instead of "you were." "Did it ever strike
you," said a friend of mine, "that whenever you hear of

a young woman found drowned she always is described as having worn elastic boots?" Such persons look at all things through a distorting medium. Important things become unimportant and *vice versâ*. The foreground is thrust back, the distance brought forward, and the middle distance is nowhere. The effect of an exaggerated praise generally is that an unfair reaction sets in. Mr. Justin M'Carthy, in his *History of Our Own Times*, points out how much the character of Lord Stratford de Redcliffe has suffered from the absurd devotion of Kinglake. Kinglake writes (he says) of Lord Stratford de Redcliffe "as if he were describing the all-compelling movements of some divinity or providence." What nonsense has been talked about Millais' landscapes, Whistler's nocturnes, Swinburne poetry—all excellent enough in their way, and requiring to be praised according to their merits, with a reserve as to their faults. The practice of puffing tends to destroy all sort of proportion in criticism. When single sentences or portions of sentences of apparently unqualified praise are detached from context, and heaped together so as to induce the public to think that all praise and no blame has been awarded, of course all proportion is lost. Macaulay lashed this vice in his celebrated essay on Robert Montgomery's poems. "We expect some reserve," he says, "some decent pride in our hatter and our bootmaker. But no artifice by which notoriety can be obtained is thought too abject for a man of letters. Extreme poverty may indeed in some degree be an excuse for employing these shifts as it may be an excuse for stealing a leg of mutton."

Upon the other hand, how unfair is exaggerated

blame. I am not speaking here of that which is in-
tentionally unfair, but of blame fairly meant and in
some degree deserved, but where the language is out
of all proportion to the offence.

Ruskin so belaboured the poor ancients about their
landscapes that when I was a youth he had taught me to
believe that Claude and Ruisdael were mere duffers.
So when he speaks of Whistler, as we shall presently see,
his blame is so exaggerated that it produces a revulsion
in the mind of the reader. He said Whistler's painting
consisted in throwing a pot of paint in the public's face.
Well! we may say Whistler is somewhat sketchy and
careless or wanting in colour, but it is quite possible to
keep our tempers over it.

"This salad is very gritty," said a gentleman to
Douglas Jerrold at a dinner party. "Gritty," said
Jerrold, "it's a mere gravel path with a few weeds in
it." That was very unfair on the salad.

3. *Criticism should be appropriate.*

I mean by this something different from proportionate.
Sometimes the language of criticism is not that of exag·
geration, but yet it is quite as inappropriate. The critic
may have taken his seat too high or too low for a proper
survey, or he may, by want of education or by careless-
ness, use quite the wrong words to express his meaning.
You will hear a man say, "I was enchanted with the
Biglow Papers," or "I was charmed with the hyenas at
the Zoological Gardens." I think one of the distinguish-
ing characteristics of a gentleman, and what makes the
society of educated gentlemen so pleasant, is that their
language is appropriate without effort. "'What a
delicious shiver is creeping over those limes!' said

Lancelot, half to himself. The expression struck
Argemone; it was the right one." This is what makes
some people's conversation so interesting. It is full of
appropriate language. This is perhaps even more the
case with educated ladies. I think it is Macaulay who
says that the ordinary letter of an English lady is the
best English style to be found anywhere.

"It would be bad *grammar*," said Cobbett, "to say of
the House of Commons, 'It is a sink of iniquity, and
they are a set of rascally swindlers.'" Of course, the bad
grammar is almost immaterial. The expression is either
a gross libel or a lamentable fact. "If a man," said
Sydney Smith, "were to kill the minister and church-
wardens of his parish nobody would accuse him of want
of taste. The Scythians always ate their grandfathers ;
they behaved very respectfully to them for a long time,
but as soon as their grandfathers became old and
troublesome, and began to tell long stories, they immediately ate them; nothing could be more *improper*
and even *disrespectful* than dining off such near and
venerable relations, yet we could not with any propriety
accuse them of bad taste." This is very humorous. To
say that it is improper or disrespectful is as absurd as to
say that it is bad taste. It is properly described as cruel,
revolting, and abominable.

Not being at all a French scholar, and coming suddenly in view of Mont Blanc, I ventured to say to my
guide, "*C'est très joli.*" "*Non, Monsieur,*" said he,
"*ce n'est pas joli, mais c'est curieux à voir.*" I think we
were both of us rather out of it that time.

I remember an old lady of my acquaintance pointing
to her new chintz of peonies and sunflowers, and asking

me if I did not think it was very "chaste." I should like to have said, "Oh, yes, very, quite rococo," but I daren't.

The wife of a clergyman, writing to the papers about the "Penge Mystery," said that certain of the parties (whom most right-minded people thought had committed most atrocious crimes, if not actual murder) had been guilty of a breach of "les convenances de société." This is almost equal to De Quincey's friend, who committed a murder, which at the time he thought little about. Keble said to Froude, "Froude, you said you thought Law's *Serious Call* was a clever book; it seemed to me as if you had said the Day of Judgment will be a pretty sight."

I ought here to mention the use, or rather misuse, of words which are often called "slang," such as "awfully jolly," "fearfully tedious," "horribly dull," or the expression "quite alarming," which young ladies, I think, have now happily forgotten, and the equally silly use of the word "howling" by young men. Such expressions mean absolutely nothing, and are destructive of intelligent conversation. A man was being tried for a serious assault, and had used a violent and coarse expression towards the prosecutor. "You must be careful not to be misled by the bad language reported to have been used by the prisoner," said the judge. "You will find from the evidence that he has applied the same expression to his best friend, to a glass of beer, to his grandmother, his boots, and his own eyes."

4. *Criticism should be strong.*

I hope from the remarks I have previously made it will not be supposed that I think all criticism should be of a flat, neutral tint, or what may be called the washy

order. On the contrary, if criticism is not strong it
cannot lift a young genius out of the struggling crowd,
and it cannot beat down some bumptious impostor. If
the critic really believes that a new poet writes like
Milton, or a new artist paints like Sir Joshua, let him
say so; or if he thinks any work vile or contemptible,
let him say so ; but let him say so well. Mere exaggerated language, as we have seen, is not strength; but
if there is real strength in the criticism, and it is proportionate and appropriate, it will effect its purpose. It
will free the genius, or it will crush the humbug. A
good critic should be feared :

> "Good Lord, I wouldn't have that man
> Attack me in the *Times*,"

was said of Jacob Omnium.

> "Yes, I am proud, I own it, when I see
> Men not afraid of God afraid of me,"

Pope said, and I can fancy with what a stern joy an
honest critic would arise and slay what he believed to
be false and vicious. In no time was the need of strong
criticism greater than it is at present. The press is
teeming with rubbish and something worse. Everybody
reads anything that is published with sufficient flourish
and advertisement, and those who read have mostly no
power of judging for themselves, nor would they be turned
from the garbage which seems to delight them by any
gentle persuasion. It is therefore most necessary that
the critic should speak out plainly and boldly, though with
temper and discretion. I suppose we have all of us read
Lord Macaulay's criticism upon Robert Montgomery's
poems. The poems are, of course, forgotten ; but the

essay still lives as a specimen of the terribly slashing style. This is the way one couplet is dealt with—

> "The soul aspiring pants its source to mount,
> As streams meander level with their fount."

"We take this on the whole to be the worst similitude in the world. In the first place, no stream meanders, or can possibly meander, level with its fount. In the next place, if streams did meander level with their founts, no two motions can be less like each other than that of meandering level and that of mounting upwards. After saying that lightning is designless and self-created, he says, a few lines further on, that it is the Deity who bids

> 'the thunder rattle from the skiey deep.'

His theory is therefore this, that God made the thunder but the lightning made itself." Of course, poor Robert Montgomery was crushed flat, and rightly. Yet before this essay was written his poems had a larger circulation than Southey or Coleridge, just as in our own time Martin Tupper had a larger sale than Tennyson or Browning. Fancy if Tupper had been treated in the same vein how the following lines would have fared :—

> "Weep, relentless eye of Nature,
> Drop some pity on the soil,
> Every plant and every creature
> Droops and faints in dusty toil."

What do the plants toil at? I thought we knew they toil not, neither do they spin. It goes on—

> "Then the cattle and the flowers
> Yet shall raise their drooping heads,
> And, refreshed by plenteous showers,
> Lie down joyful in their beds."

Whether the flowers are to lie down in the cattle beds or the cattle are to lie down in the flower beds does not perhaps distinctly appear, but I venture to think that either catastrophe is not so much to be desired as the poet seems to imagine.

In the Diary of Jeames yellowplush a couplet of Lord Lytton's *Sea Captain* is thus dealt with—

> "Girl, beware,
> The love that trifles round the charms ît gilds
> Oft ruins while it shines."

"Igsplane this men and angels! I've tried every way, back'ards, for'ards, and in all sorts of tranceposishons as thus—

> The love that ruins round the charms it shines
> Gilds while it trifles oft,

or
> The charm that gilds around the love it ruins
> Oft trifles while it shines,

or
> The ruin that love gilds and shines around
> Oft trifles while it charms,

or
> Love while it charms, shines round and ruins oft
> The trifles that it gilds,

or
> The love that trifles, gilds, and ruins oft
> While round the charms it shines.

All which are as sensable as the fust passidge."

Dryden added coarseness to strength in his remarks when he wrote of one of Settle's plays :—" To conclude this act with the most rumbling piece of nonsense spoken yet—

> 'To flattering lightning our feigned smiles conform,
> Which, backed with thunder, do but gild a storm.'

Conform a smile to lightning, make a smile imitate lightning; lightning sure is a threatening thing. And this lightning must gild a storm; and gild a storm by being backed by thunder. So that here is gilding by conforming, smiling lightning, backing and thundering. I am mistaken if nonsense is not here pretty thick sown. Sure the poet writ these two lines aboard some smack in a storm, and, being sea-sick, spewed up a good lump of clotted nonsense at once." Dryden wrote in a fit of rage and spite, and it is not necessary to be vulgar in order to be strong; but it is really a good thing to expose in plain language the meandering nonsense which, unless detected, is apt to impose upon careless readers, and so to encourage writers in their bad habits.

A young friend of mine imagined that he could make his fame as a painter. Holding one of his pictures before his father, and his father saying it was roughly and carelessly done, he said, "No, but, father, look; it looks better if I hold it further off." "Yes, Charlie, the further you hold it off the better it looks." That was severe, but strong and just. The young man had no real genius for painting, and his father knew it.

It must be remembered that criticism cannot be strong unless it be the real opinion of the writer. If the critic is hampered by endeavouring to make his own views square with those of the writer, or the publisher, or the public, he cannot speak out his mind, but is half-hearted in his work.

5. *Natural.*

Criticism should be natural, that is, not too artificial. This is a somewhat difficult matter upon which to lay down any rules; but one often feels what a terrible thing

B

it is when one wants to admire something to be told,
"Oh, but the unities are not preserved," or this or that
is quite inadmissible by all the rules of art.

"Hallo ! you chairman, here's sixpence ; do step into
that bookseller's shop, and call me a day-tall critic. I
am very willing to give any of them a crown to help me
with his tackling to get my father and my uncle Toby off
the stairs, and to put them to bed."

"And how did Garrick speak the soliloquy last
night?" "Oh, against all rule, my lord, most un-
grammatically ! Betwixt the substantive and the adjec-
tive, which should agree together in number, case, and
gender, he made a breach thus— stopping as if the point
wanted settling ; and betwixt the nominative case, which
your lordship knows should govern the verb, he suspended his voice a dozen times, three seconds, and three
fifths, by a stop watch, my lord, each time." Admirable
grammarian ! "But, in suspending his voice, was the
sense suspended likewise? Did no expression of atti-
tude or countenance fill up the chasm? Was the eye
silent?   Did you narrowly look ?"   "I looked only
at the stop watch, my lord." Excellent observer !
"And what about this new book that the whole world
makes such a rout about ?"   "Oh, it is out of all plumb,
my lord, quite an irregular thing ! Not one of the angles
at the four corners was a right angle. I had my rule and
compasses, my lord, in my pocket." Excellent critic !
"And for the epic poem your lordship bid me look at ;
upon taking the length, breadth, height, and depth of it,
and trying them at home upon an exact scale of Bossu's,
'tis out, my lord, in every one of its dimensions." Admirable connoisseur ! "And did you step in to take a look at

the grand picture on your way back." "It is a melancholy
daub! my lord, not one principle of the pyramid in any one
group; there is nothing of the colouring of Titian, the
expression of Rubens, the grace of Raphael, the purity
of Domenichino, the corregiescity of Corregio, the learning of Poussin, the airs of Guido, the taste of the Caraccis,
or the grand contour of Angelo." "Grant me patience,
just heaven! Of all the cants which are canted in this
canting world, though the cant of hypocrites may be the
worst—the cant of criticism is the most tormenting! I
would go fifty miles on foot, for I have not a horse
worth riding on, to kiss the hand of that man whose
generous heart will give up the reins of his imaginations
into his author's hands; be pleased, he knows not why,
and cares not wherefore. Great Apollo! if thou art in a
giving humour, give me—I ask no more—but one stroke
of native humour with a single spark of thy own fire
along with it, and send Mercury with the rules and compasses if he can be spared, with my compliments, to——
no matter."

This is all very amusing, and I don't know that the
case upon that side could be better stated, except that
it is overstated; for, if this be true, there ought to be no
such thing as criticism at all, and all rules are worse than
useless. Everybody may do as he pleases. And yet we
know that not only is there a right way and a wrong of
painting a picture, writing a book, making a building, or
composing a symphony, but there are rules which, if dis-
obeyed, will destroy the work. These rules, apparently
artificial, have their foundation in nature, and were first
dictated by her. Only we must be careful still to appeal
constantly to her as the source and fountain of our rules.

" First follow nature, and your judgment frame
By her just standard, which is still the same,
Unerring nature, still divinely bright,
One clear, unchanged, and universal light,
Life, force, and beauty must to all impart,
At once the source, and end, and test of art."

By too much attention to theory, by too close a study
of books, we may become narrow-minded and pedantic,
and gradually may become unable to appreciate natural
beauties, our whole attention being concentrated on the
defects in art. We want to listen to the call of the
poet,

" Come forth into the light of things,
Let nature be your teacher."

It is nature that mellows and softens the distance, and
brings out sharply the lights and shadows of the foreground, and the artist must follow her if he would
succeed. It is nature who warbles softly in the love
notes of the bird, and who elevates the soul by the roar
of the cataract and the pealing of the thunder. To her
the musician and the poet listen, and imitate the great
teacher. It is nature who, in the structure of the leaf or
in the avenue of the lofty limes, teaches the architect
how to adorn his designs with the most graceful of em-
bellishments, to rear the lofty column or display the
lengthening vista of the cathedral aisle. It is nature
who is teaching us all to be tender, loving, and true, and
to love and worship God, and to admire all His works.
Let us then in our criticism refer everything first of all to
nature. Is the work natural? Does it follow nature?
Secondly, does it follow the rules of art. If it passes
the first test, it is well worth the courteous attention of

the critic. If it passes both tests, it is perfect. But if only the second test is passed, it may please a few pedants, but it is worthless, and cannot live.

6. *Criticisms should be bonâ fide.*

You will be rather alarmed at a lawyer beginning this topic, and will expect to hear pages of "Starkie on Libel," or to have all the perorations of Erskine's speeches recited to you. For one terrible moment I feel I have you in my power; but I scorn to take advantage of the position. I don't mean to talk about libel at all, or, at least, not more than I can help. I have been endeavouring to show what good criticism should be like. If criticism is so base that there is a question to be left to a jury as to what damages ought to be paid for the speaking or writing of it, one may say at once that it is unworthy of the name of criticism at all. Slander is not criticism. But there is a great deal of criticism which may be called not *bonâ fide*, which is yet not malicious. It is biassed perhaps, even from some charitable motive, perhaps from some sordid motive, perhaps from indolence, from a desire to be thought learned or clever, or what not—in fact, from one or other of those thousand things which prevent persons from speaking fairly and straightforwardly. When you take up the *Athenæum* or the *Spectator*, and read from those very able reviews an account of the last new novel, do you think the writer has written simply what he truly thinks and feels about the matter? No! he has been told he has been dull of late. He feels he must write a spicy review. He has a cold in his head, he is savage accordingly. A friend of his tells him he knows the author, or he recognizes the

name of a college friend—he will be lenient. The
book is on a subject which he meant to take up himself; and, without knowing it, he is jealous. I need
not multiply further these suggestions which will occur
to anyone. We all remember the dinner in Paternoster
Row given by Mrs. Bungay, the publisher's wife.
Bungay and Bacon are at daggers drawn; each married
the sister of the other, and they were for some time
the closest friends and partners. Since they have
separated it is a furious war between the two publishers, and no sooner does one bring out a book of
travels or poems, but the rival is in the field with
something similar. We all remember the delight of
Mrs. Bungay when the Hon. Percy Popjoy drives up
in a private hansom with an enormous grey cab horse
and a tiger behind, and Mrs. Bacon is looking out
grimly from the window on the opposite side of the
street. "In the name of commonsense, Mr. Pendennis,"
Shandon asked, "what have you been doing—praising
one of Mr. Bacon's books? Bungay has been with me
in a fury this morning at seeing a laudatory article
upon one of the works of the odious firm over the
way." Pen's eyes opened wide with astonishment.
"Do you mean to say," he asked, "that we are to
praise no books that Bacon publishes; or that if the
books are good we are to say that they are bad?"
Pen says, "I would rather starve, by Jove, and never
earn another penny by my pen, than strike an opponent
an unfair blow, or if called upon to place him, rank him
below his honest desert."

There was a trial in London in December, 1878,
which illustrates the subject I am upon. It was an

action for libel by the well-known artist, Mr. Whistler, against Mr. Ruskin, the most distinguished art critic of the age. The passage in the writing of Mr. Ruskin, of which Mr. Whistler complained, contains, I think, almost every fault which, according to my divisions, a criticism can contain. The passage is as follows :—
" For Mr. Whistler's own sake no less than for the protection of the purchaser, Sir Coutts Lindsey ought not to have admitted works into the gallery in which the ill-educated conceit of the artist so nearly approached the aspect of wilful imposture. I have seen and heard much of cockney impudence before now, but never ex-pected to hear a coxcomb ask 200 guineas for flinging a pot of paint in the public's face."

The Attorney-General of the day, as counsel for Mr. Ruskin, said that this was a severe and slashing criticism, but perfectly fair and *bonâ fide*.

Now, let us see. First, there is the expression, "the ill-educated conceit of the artist nearly approached the aspect of wilful imposture." That may be severe and slashing, but is it fair? If there *was* a wilful imposition, why not say so; but, of course, there was not, and could not be ; but it is most unfair to insinuate that there nearly was. The truth is, the words "wilful imposture" are a gross exaggeration. The jury, after retiring, came into court and asked the judge what was the meaning of wilful imposture, and, being told that it meant nothing in particular, they returned a verdict of damages one farthing, which meant to say that they thought equally little of Whistler's picture and of Ruskin's criticism. Next we come to "Cockney impudence" and "cox-comb." Surely these terms must be grossly inappro-

priate to the subject in hand, which is Whistler's
painting, and not his personal qualities. Next, it seems
that Mr. Ruskin thinks it is an offence to ask 200
guineas for a picture, but where the offence lies we are
not told. It might be folly to *give* 200 guineas for
one of Whistler's pictures, but why should he be
abused for asking it? The insinuation is that it is a
false pretence, and such an insinuation is not *bonâ
fide.* Lastly, we are told that Mr. Whistler has been
flinging a pot of paint in the public's face. In the first
place, this is vulgar. In the next place, it is absurd.
When Sydney Smith said that someone's writing was
like a spider having escaped from the inkstand and
wandered over the paper, it was an exaggerated criticism, but it was appropriate. But if Mr. Whistler flung
a pot of paint anywhere, it was upon his own canvas,
and not into the face of the public. Now, let anybody
think what is the effect of such criticism. Is one enabled
by the light of it to see the merits or faults of Whistler's
painting? And yet this was written by the greatest art
critic in this country, by the man who has done more to
reveal the secrets of Nature and of Art to us all than
any man living, and, I had almost said, than any living
or dead. But passion and arrogance are not criticism;
and, in the sense in which I have used the term, such
criticism is not *bonâ fide.* Well may Mr. Matthew
Arnold say, speaking of Mr. Ruskin's criticism upon
another subject, that he forgets all moderation and
proportion, and loses the balance of his mind. This, he
says, "is to show in one's criticism to the highest excess
the note of provinciality."

There was, once upon a time, a very strong Court of

Appeal. It was universally acknowledged to be so, and the memory of it still remains, and very old lawyers still love to recall its glories. It was composed of Lord Chancellor Campbell and the Lords Justices Knight-Bruce and Turner. Bethell (afterwards Lord Westbury) was an ambitious and aspiring man, and was always most caustic in his criticisms. He had been arguing before the above Court one day, and upon his turning round after finishing his argument, some counsel in the row behind him asked, "Well, Bethell, how will their judgment go?" Bethell replied, in his softest but most cutting tones, "I do not know. Knight-Bruce is a jack-pudding. Turner is an old woman. And no human being can by any possibility predict what will fall from the lips of that inexpressibly fatuous individual who sits in the middle." This is funny, but it is vulgar, and it is not given in good faith. It is the offspring of anger and spite mixed with a desire to be clever and antithetical.

I gather from Mr. Matthew Arnold's essays on criticism that the endeavour of the critic should be to see the object criticized "as in itself it really is," or as in another passage he says, "Real criticism obeys an instinct prompting it to know the best that is known and thought in the world." "In order to do or to be this, criticism," he says, in italics, "ought to be *disinterested.*" He points out how much English criticism is not disinterested. He says, "We have the *Edinburgh Review*, existing as an organ of the old Whigs, and for as much play of mind as may suit its being *that;* we have the *Quarterly Review*, existing as an organ of the Tories, and for as much play of mind as may suit its being that; we have the *British Quarterly Review*, existing as an organ of the political Dissenters, and for as much play of mind as may suit its being that; we have the *Times* existing as an organ of the common satisfied well-to-do Englishman, and for as much play of mind as may suit its being that. . . . Directly this play of mind wants to have more scope, and to forget the pressure of practical considerations a little, it is checked, it is made to feel the chain. We saw this the other day in the extinction so much to be regretted of the *Home and Foreign Review;* perhaps in no organ of criticism was there so much knowledge, so much play of mind; but these could not save it. It must needs be that men should act in sects and parties, that each of these sects and parties should have its organ, and should make this organ subserve the interest of its action; but it would be well too that there should be a criticism, not the minister of those interests, nor their enemy, but absolutely and entirely independent of them. No other criticism will ever attain any real authority, or make any real way towards its end,—the creating a current of true and fresh ideas."

This, it must be remembered, was written in 1865. Would Mr. Matthew Arnold be .happier now with the *Fortnightly* and the *Nineteenth Century* and others? There is, I think, a good deal of truth in the passage I have just quoted. I think he might have allowed that, among so many writers, each advocating his own view or the view of his party or sect, we ought to have some chance of forming a judgment. A question seems to get a fair chance of being

> "Set in all lights by many minds
> To close the interests of all."

But, as I said, there is a good deal in what the writer says. The *Daily News* says the Government is all wrong, and the *Daily Telegraph* says it is all right; and if any paper ventured to be moderate it would go to the wall in a week. I think what he says is true, but there is no occasion to be so angry about it. We really are very thankful for such men as Carlyle, Ruskin, and Matthew Arnold, and I can't help thinking they have had their proper share of praise, and have had their share of influence upon their age. The air of neglected superiority, which they assume, detracts not a little from the pleasure with which one always reads them.

Perhaps some of my conservative friends will regret the good old times in which criticism was really criticism, when a book had to run the gauntlet of a few well established critics of *the* club, or a play was applauded or damned by a select few in the front row of the pit. I agree to lament a past which can never return, but, on the whole, I think we are the gainers. Also, I very much incline to think that the standard of criticism is higher now than in the very palmy days when Addison wrote, or when the *Edinburgh* or *Quarterly* were first started. I incline to agree with Leslie Stephen in his *Hours in a Library*, that, if most of the critical articles of even Jeffrey and Mackintosh were submitted to a modern editor, he would reject them as inadequate; but I think that perhaps they excel our modern efforts in a certain reserve and dignity, and in a more matured thoughtfulness.

If criticism is an art, such as I have described it, and is subject to certain rules and conditions; if good criticism is appreciative, proportionate, appropriate, strong, natural, and *bonâ fide*, and bad criticism is the reverse of all this, why, you will ask, cannot the art be taught by some School or Academy ; and if criticism is so important a matter as you say, surely the State might see to it? I must own I am against it. Mr. Matthew Arnold, who is much in favour of founding an academy, which is not only to judge of original works but of the criticisms of others upon them, states the matter very fairly. He says, " So far as routine and authority tend to embarrass energy and inventive genius, academies may be said to be obstructive to energy and inventive genius ; and, to this extent, to the human spirit's general advance. But then this evil is so much compensated by the propagation on a large scale of the mental aptitudes and demands, which an open mind and a flexible intelligence naturally engender; genius itself in the long run so greatly finds its account in this propaga-tion, and bodies like the French Academy have such power for promoting it, that the general advance of the human spirit is perhaps, on the whole, rather furthered than im-peded by their existence."

But I do not accede to this opinion. It is under the free open air of heaven, in the wild woods and the meadows that the loveliest and sweetest flowers bloom, and not in the trim gardens or the hot-houses, and even in our gardens in England we strive to preserve some lingering traits of the open country. I believe that just as the gift of freedom to the masses of our countrymen teaches them to use that freedom with care and intelligence, just as the abolition of tests and oaths makes men loyal and trustworthy, so it is well to have freedom in literature and criticism. Mistakes will be made and mischief done, but in the

long run the effect of a keen competition, and an advancing public taste will tell. I don't hesitate to assert,
without fear of contradiction, that critical art has im-
proved rapidly during the last twenty years in this country, where a man is free to start a critical review, and
to write about anybody, or anything, and in any manner,
provided he keeps within the law. He is only restrained
by the competition of others, and by the public taste,
which are both constantly increasing. No doubt an
author will write with greater spirit, and with greater
decorum, if he knows that his merits are sure to be
fairly acknowledged, and his faults certain to ·be accu-
rately noted. But this object may be attained, I believe,
without an academy. On the other hand, what danger
there is in an academy becoming cliquey, nay even cor-
rupt. We have an academy here in the painting art, but
except that it collects within its walls every year a vaster
number of daubs than it is possible for any one ever to
see with any degree of comfort, I don't know what particular use it is of. As a school or college it may be of
use, but as a critical academy it does very little.

I have thus endeavoured to show what I mean by
my six divisions of criticism, and I have no doubt you
will all of you have divined that my six divisions are
capable of being expressed in one word, Criticism must
be *true.* To be true, it must be appreciative, or understanding, it must be in due proportion, it must be appropriate, it must be strong, it must be natural, it must be
bonâ fide. There is nothing which an Englishman hates
so much as being false. Our great modern poet, in one
of his strongest lines, says—

" This is a shameful thing for men to lie."

And he speaks of Wellington—

> " Truth teller was our England's Alfred named,
> Truth lover was our English Duke."

Emerson notices that many of our phrases turn upon
this love of truth, such as " The English of this is,"
" Honour bright," " His word is as good as his bond."

> " 'Tis not enough taste, learning, judgment join ;
> In all you speak let truth, and candour shine."

I am certain that if men and women would believe that
it is important that they should form a true judgment
upon things, and that they should speak or write it when
required, we should get rid of a great deal of bad art,
bad books, bad pictures, bad buildings, bad music, and
bad morals.   I am further certain that by constantly
uttering false criticisms we perpetuate such things.   And
what harm we are doing to our own selves in the mean-
time !   How habitually warped, how unsteady, how
feeble, the judgment becomes, which is not kept bright
and vigorous through right use.   How insensibly we
become callous or indolent about forming a correct
judgment.   "It is a pleasure to stand upon the shore
and see the ships tossed upon the sea; a pleasure to
stand in the window of a castle and to see a battle and
the adventures thereof below : but no pleasure is com-
parable to the standing upon the vantage ground of
truth (a hill not to be commanded and where the air
is always clear and serene) and to see the errors and
wanderings and mists and tempests in the vale below, so
always that this prospect be with pity and not with
swelling or pride.   Certainly it is heaven upon earth to
have a man's mind move in charity, rest in Providence,
and turn upon the poles of truth."

In conclusion, I am aware that I have treated the subject most inadequately, and that others have treated the same subject with much more power; but I am satisfied of the great importance of a right use of the critical faculty, and I think it may be that my mode of treatment may arrest the attention of some minds which are apt to be frightened at a learned method, and may induce them to take more heed of the judgments which they are hourly passing on a great variety of subjects. If we still persist in saying when some one jingles some jig upon the piano that it is "charming," if we say of every daub in the Academy that it is "lovely," if every new building or statue is pronounced "awfully jolly," if the fastidious rubbish of the last volume of poetry is "grand," if the slip-shod grammar of the last new novel is "quite sweet," when shall we see an end of these bad things. And observe further, these bad things live on and affect the human mind for ever. Bad things are born of bad. Who can tell what may be the effect of seeing day by day an hideous building, of hearing day by day indifferent music, of constantly reading a lot of feeble twaddle? Surely one effect will be that we shall gradually lose our appreciation of what is good and beautiful. "A thing of beauty is a joy for ever." Ah! but we must have eyes to see it. This springtime is lovely, if we have the eyes to see it; but, if we have not, its loveliness is nothing to us, and if we miss seeing it we shall have dimmer eyes to see it next year and the next; and if we cannot now see beauty and truth through the glass darkly, we shall be unable to gaze on them when we come to see them face to face.

II.   ON LUXURY.

AN eminent lawyer of my acquaintance had a Socratic
habit of interrupting the conversation by saying, "Let us
understand one another : when you say so-and-so, do you
mean so-and-so, or something quite different." Now,
although it is intolerable that the natural flow of social
intercourse should be thus impeded, yet in writing a
paper to be laid before a learned and fastidious society
one is bound to let one's hearers a little into the secret,
and to state fairly what the subject of the essay really is.
I suppose we shall all admit that bad luxury is bad, and
good luxury is good, unless the phrase good luxury is a
contradiction in terms.   We must try to avoid disputing
about words.   The word luxury, according to its deriva-
tion, signifies an extravagant and outrageous indulgence
of the appetites or desires.   If we take this as the meaning of the word, we shall agree that luxury is bad ; but if
we take luxury to be only another name for the refine-
ments of civilization, we shall all approve of it.   But the
real and substantial question is not what the word means,
but, what is that thing which we all agree is bad or good;
where does the bad begin and the good end ; how are
we to discern the difference ; and how are we to avoid
the one and embrace the other.   In this essay, therefore,
I intend to use the word luxury to denote that indul-

gence which interferes with the full and proper exercise of all the faculties, powers, tastes, and whatever is good and worthy in a man. Enjoyments, relaxations, delights, indulgences which are beneficial, I do not denominate " luxury." All indulgences which fit us for our duties are good; all which tend to unfit us for them are bad; and these latter I call luxuries. Some one will say, perhaps, that some indulgences are merely indifferent, and produce no appreciable effect upon body or mind; and it might be enough to dismiss such things with the maxim, " *de minimis non curat lex.*" But the doctrine is dangerous, and I doubt if anything in this world is absolutely immaterial. De Quincey mentions the case of a man who committed a murder, which at the time he thought little about, but he was led on from that to gambling and Sabbath breaking. Probably in this weary world any indulgence or pleasure which is not bad is not indifferent, but absolutely good. The world is not so bright, so comfortable, so pleasant, that we can afford to scorn the good the gods provide us. In Mr. Reade's book on *Study and Stimulants,* Matthew Arnold says, a moderate use of wine adds to the agreeableness of life, and whatever adds to the agreeableness of life, adds to its resources and powers. There cannot be a doubt that the bodily frame is capable of being wearied, and that it needs repose and refreshment, and this is a law which a man trifles with at his peril. The same is true of the intellectual and moral faculties. They claim rest and refreshment; they must have comfort and pleasure or they will begin to flag. It must also be always remembered that in the every-day work of this world the body and the mind have to go through a great deal which is

c

depressing and taxing to the energy, and a certain
amount of "set off" is required to keep the balance
even. We must remember this especially with respect
to the poor. Pipes and cigars may be a luxury to the
idle and rich, but we ought not to grudge a pipe to a
poor man who is overworked and miserable. Some
degree of comfort we all feel to be at times essential
when we have a comfortless task to perform. With good
food and sleep, for instance, we can get through the
roughest work ; with the relaxation of pleasant society
we can do the most tedious daily work. If, on the other
hand, we are worried and uncomfortable, we become un-
fitted for our business. We all have our troubles to
contend against, and we require comfort, relaxation,
stimulation of some sort to help us in the battle. There
are certain duties which most of us have to perform, and
which, to use a common expression, "take it out of us."
Thus most of us are compelled to travel more or less.
An old gentleman travelling by coach on a long journey
wished to sleep off the tediousness of the night, but his
travelling companion woke him up every ten minutes
with the inquiry, " Well, sir, how are you by this." At
last the old gentleman's patience was fairly tired out.
" I was very well when I got into the coach, and I'm
very well now, and if any change takes place I'll let you
know." I was coming from London to Beckenham, and
in the carriage with me was a gentleman quietly and
attentively reading the newspaper. A lady opposite to
him, whenever we came to a station, cried out, " Oh,
what station's this, what station's this ?" Being told, she
subsided, more or less, till the next station. · The gentleman's patience was at last exhausted. " If there is any

particular station at which you wish to alight I will inform you when we arrive."

Such are some of the annoying circumstances of travel. Then, at the end of the journey, are we sure of a comfortable night's rest? It was a rule upon circuit that the barristers arriving at an inn had the choice of bedrooms according to seniority, and woe betide the junior who dared to infringe the rule and endeavour to secure by force or fraud the best bedroom. The leaders, who had the hardest work to do, required the best night's rest. A party of barristers arrived late one night at their accustomed inn, a half-way house to the next assize town, and found one of the best bedrooms already occupied. They were told by some wag that it was occupied by a young man just joined the circuit. There was a rush to the bedroom. The culprit was dragged out of bed and deposited on the floor. A venerable old gentleman in a nightcap and gown addressed the ring- leader of his assailants, Serjeant Golbourne, "Brother Golbourne, brother Golbourne, is this the way to treat a Christian judge?" I should not have liked to have been one of those who had to conduct a cause before him next day. Who can be generous, benevolent, kindly, and even-tempered if one is to be subjected to such harassing details as I have above narrated? and I have no doubt that a fair amount of comfort is necessary to the exercise of the Christian virtues. I am not at all sure that pilgrims prayed any better because they had peas in their shoes, and it is well known that soldiers fight best when they are well fed. A certain amount of comfort and pleasure is good for us, and is refreshing to body and spirit. Such things, for instance, as the bath

in the morning ; the cup of warm tea or coffee for break-
fast ; the glass of beer or wine and variety of food at
dinner ; the rest or nap in the arm-chair or sofa ; an
occasional novel ; the pipe before going to bed ; the
change of dress ; music or light reading in the evening ;
even the night-cap recommended by Mr. Banting ; games
of chance or skill ; dancing ;—surely such things may
renovate, soothe, and render more elastic and vigorous
both body and mind.

While, therefore, I have admitted fully that we all
require "sweetness and light," that some indulgence is
necessary for the renovation of our wearied souls and
bodies ; yet it very often will happen that the thing in
which we desire to indulge does not tend at all in this
direction, or it may be that, although a moderate indulgence does so tend, an immoderate use has precisely
the reverse effect. My subject, therefore, divides itself,
firstly, into a consideration of those luxuries which are
per se deleterious, and those which are so only by
excessive use.

I suppose you will not be surprised to hear that I
think we are in danger, in the upper and middle
classes at all events, of going far beyond the point
where pleasures and indulgences tend to the improvement of body and mind. Surely there are many of
us who can remember when the habits of our fathers
were less luxurious than they are now. In a leading
article in a newspaper not long ago the writer said,
"All classes without exception spend too much on
what may be called luxuries. A very marked change
in this respect has been noticed by every one who
studies the movements of society. Among people

whose fathers regarded champagne as a devout Aryan
might have regarded the Soma juice—viz., as a beverage
reserved for the gods and for millionaires—the foaming
grape of Eastern France is now habitually consumed.
. . ." He goes on, "The luxuries of the poor are
few, and chiefly consist of too much beer, and of little
occasional dainties. What pleasures but the grossest
does the State provide for the artisan's leisure?" "It
does not do," says the writer, "to be hard upon them,
but it is undeniable that this excess of expenditure on
what in no sense profits them is enormous in the mass."

Not long ago a great outcry was heard about the
extravagance and luxury of the working man. It was
stated often, and certainly not without foundation, that
the best of everything in the markets in the way of food
was bought at the highest prices by workmen or their
wives; and although the champagne was not perhaps so
very freely indulged in, nor so pure as might be wished,
yet, that the working men indulged themselves in more
drink than was good for their stomachs, and in more expensive drinks than was good for their purses, no man
can doubt.

If this increase of luxury is observable in the lower
classes, how much more easily can it be discerned in the
middle classes. Take for instance the pleasures of the
table. I do not speak of great entertainments or life in
palaces or great houses, which do not so much vary
from one age to another, but of the ordinary life of
people like ourselves. Spenser says :—

> "The antique world excess and pryde did hate,
> Such proud luxurious pomp is swollen up of late."

How many more dishes and how many more wines do

we put on the table than our ancestors afforded. Pope
writes of Balaam's housekeeping :—.

> " A single dish the week day meal affords,
>   An added pudding solemnized the Lord's. "

Then when he became rich :—

> " Live like yourself was soon my lady's word,
>   And lo, two puddings smoked upon the board ! "

Then his description of his own table is worth noting :—·

> "Content with little, I can manage here
> On brocoli and mutton round the year,
> 'Tis true no turbots dignify my boards,
> But gudgeons, flounders, what my Thames affords.
>
> To Hounslow Heath I point, and Banstead Down ;
> Thence comes your mutton, and these chicks my own,
> From yon old walnut tree a show'r shall fall,
> And grapes, long lingering on my only wall,
> And figs from standard and espalier join—
> The deuce is in you if you cannot dine. "

Now, however, the whole world is put under contribution
to supply our daily meals, and the palate is being constantly stimulated, and in some degree impaired by a
variety of food and wine. And I am sure that the
effect of this is to produce a distaste for wholesome
food. I daresay we have all heard of the Scotchman
who had drunk too much whisky. He said, " I can't
drink water; it turns sae acid on the stomach." This
increase of the luxuries of the table, beyond what was
the habit of our fathers, is shown chiefly, I think,
when we are at home and alone ; but if one is visiting
or entertaining others, how often is one perfectly bored
by the quantity of food and drink which is handed
round. Things in season and out of season, perhaps ill

assorted, ill cooked, cold, and calculated to make one extremely ill, but no doubt costing a great deal of money, time, and anxiety to the givers of the feast. Then we fall to grumbling, and are discontented with having too much, but having acquired a habit of expecting it we grumble still more if there is not as much as usual provided.

> " He knows to live, who keeps the middle state,
> And neither leans on this side or on that ;
> Nor stops, for one bad cork, his butler's pay ;
> Swears, like Albutius, a good cook away ;
> Nor lets, like Nevius, every error pass—
> The musty wine, foul cloth, or greasy glass."

But what is the modern idea of a dinner?—

> " After oysters Sauterne ; then sherry, champagne,
> E'er one bottle goes comes another again ;
> Fly up, thou bold cork, to the ceiling above,
> And tell to our ears in the sounds that they love,
> How pleasant it is to have money,
> Heigh ho ;
> How pleasant it is to have money !
>
> Your Chablis is acid, away with the hock ;
> Give me the pure juice of the purple Medoc ;
> St. Peray is exquisite ; but, if you please,
> Some Burgundy just before tasting the cheese.
> So pleasant it is to have money,
> Heigh ho ;
> So pleasant it is to have money !
>
> Fish and soup and omelette and all that—but the deuce—
> There were to be woodcocks and not Charlotte Russe,
> And so suppose now, while the things go away,
> By way of a grace, we all stand up and say—
> How pleasant it is to have money,
> Heigh ho ;
> How pleasant it is to have money!

This, of course, is meant to be satirical; but no doubt many persons regard the question of "good living" as much more important than "high thinking." "My dear fellow," said Thackeray, when a dish was served at the Rocher de Cancalle, "don't let us speak a word till we have finished this dish."

> "'Mercy!' cries Helluo. 'Mercy on my soul!
> Is there no hope? Alas!—then bring the jowl.'"

A great peer, who had expended a large fortune, summoned his heir to his death-bed, and told him that he had a secret of great importance to impart to him, which might be some compensation for the injury he had done him. The secret was that crab sauce was better than lobster sauce.

"Persicos odi," " I hate all your Frenchified fuss."

> " But a nice leg of mutton, my Lucy,
>   I prithee get ready by three;
> Have it smoking, and tender, and juicy,
>   And, what better meat can there be?
> And when it has served for the master,
>   'Twill amply suffice for the maid;
> Meanwhile I will smoke my canaster,
>   And tipple my ale in the shade."

Can anything be more awful than a public dinner—the waste, the extravagance, the outrageous superfluity of everything, the enormous waste of time, the solemn gorging, as if the whole end and aim of life were turtle and venison. I do not know whether to dignify such proceedings by the name of luxury. But what shall I say of gentlemen's clubs. They are the very hotbed of luxury. By merely asking for it you obtain almost anything you require in the way of luxury. I am aware that many men at clubs live more carefully and frugally, but I am aware also that a great many acquire habits of self-indulgence which produce idleness and selfish indifference to the wants of others. In a still more pernicious fashion, I think that refreshment bars at railway stations minister to luxury; at least I am sure they foster a habit of drinking more than is necessary, or desirable; and that is one form of luxury, and a very bad one. The fellows of a Camford college are reported to have met on one occasion and voted that we do sell our chapel organ; and the next motion, carried *nem. con.*, was that we do have a dinner. As to ornaments for the dinner table what affectation and expense do we see. But in the days of Walpole it was not amiss. "The last branch of our fashion into which the close observation of nature has been introduced is our desserts. Jellies, biscuits, sugar plums, and creams have long since given way to harlequins, gondoliers, Turks, Chinese, and shepherdesses of Saxon china. Meadows of cattle spread themselves over the table. Cottages in sugar, and temples in barley sugar, pigmy Neptunes in cars of cockle shells trampling over oceans of looking glass or seas of silver tissue. Gigantic figures succeed to pigmies; and it is known that a celebrated confectioner complained that, after having prepared a middle dish of gods and goddesses eighteen feet high, his lord would not cause the ceiling of his parlour to be demolished to facilitate their entrée. *"Imaginez-vous,"* said he, *"que milord n'a pas vouler faire ôter le plafond!"*

To show how much luxurious living has increased during the present century I propose to quote a portion of that wonderfully brilliant third chapter of Macaulay's

England which we all know. Speaking of the squire
of former days, he says, "His chief serious employ-
ment was the care of his property. He examined
samples of grain, handled pigs, and, on market days,
made bargains over a tankard with drovers and hop
merchants. His chief pleasures were commonly derived
from field sports and from an unrefined sensuality. His
language and pronunciation were such as we should
now expect to hear only from the most ignorant clowns.
His oaths, coarse jests, and scurrilous terms of abuse
were uttered with the broadest accent of his province.
It was easy to discern from the first words which he
spoke whether he came from Somersetshire or Yorkshire.
He troubled himself little about decorating his abode,
and, if he attempted decoration, seldom produced anything but deformity. The litter of a farm-yard gathered
under the windows of his bed-chamber, and the cabbages
and gooseberry bushes grew close to his hall door. His
table was loaded with coarse plenty; and guests were
cordially welcomed to it. But as the habit of drinking
to excess was general in the class to which he belonged,
and as his fortune did not enable him to intoxicate large
assemblies daily-with claret or canary, strong beer was
the ordinary beverage. The quantity of beer consumed
in those days was indeed enormous. For beer was then
to the middle and lower classes not only what beer is
now, but all that wine, tea, and ardent spirits now are.
It was only at great houses or on great occasions that
foreign drink was placed on the board. The ladies of
the house, whose business it had commonly been to cook
the repast, retired as soon as the dishes were devoured,
and left the gentlemen to their ale and tobacco. The

coarse jollity of the afternoon was often prolonged till
the revellers were laid under the table."

I quote again from another portion of the same chapter in Macaulay :—" Slate has succeeded to thatch, and
brick to timber. The pavements and the lamps, the
display of wealth in the principal shops, and the luxurious
neatness of the dwellings occupied by the gentry, would,
in the seventeenth century, have seemed miraculous."
Speaking of watering-places he says :—" The gentry of
Derbyshire and of the neighbouring counties repaired to
Buxton, where they were crowded into low wooden sheds
and regaled with oatcake, and with a viand which the
hosts called mutton, but which the guests strongly sus-
pected to be dog." Of Tunbridge Wells he says—" At
present we see there a town which would, a hundred and
sixty years ago, have ranked in population fourth or fifth
among the towns in England. The brilliancy of the
shops and the luxury of the private dwellings far surpasses
anything that England could then show." At Bath "the
poor patients to whom the waters had been recommended,
lay on straw in a place which, to use the language of a
contemporary physician, was a covert rather than a
lodging. As to the comforts and luxuries to be found in
the interior of the houses at Bath by the fashionable visitors who resorted thither in search of health and amusement, we possess information more complete and minute
than generally can be obtained on such subjects. A
writer assures us that in his younger days the gentlemen
who visited the springs slept in rooms hardly as good as
the garrets which he lived to see occupied by footmen.
The floors of the dining-room were uncarpeted, and were
coloured brown with a wash made of soot and small beer

in order to hide the dirt. Not a wainscot was painted. Not a hearth or chimney piece was of marble. A slab of common freestone, and fire-irons which had cost from three to four shillings, were thought sufficient for any fireplace. The best apartments were hung with coarse woollen stuff, and were furnished with rush-bottomed chairs."

Of London Macaulay says :—"The town did not, as now, fade by imperceptible degrees into the country. No long avenues of villas, embowered in lilacs and laburnum, extended from the great source of wealth and civilization almost to the boundaries of Middlesex, and far into the heart of Kent and Surrey." In short, there was nothing like the Avenue and the Fox Grove, Beckenham, in old times, and we who live there ought to be immensely grateful for our undeserved blessings. "At present," he says, "the bankers, the merchants, and the chief shopkeepers repair to the city on six mornings of every week for the transaction of business ; but they reside in other quarters of the metropolis or suburban country seats, surrounded by shrubberies and flower gardens." Again, "If the most fashionable parts of the capital could be placed before us, such as they then were, we should be disgusted by their squalid appearance, and poisoned by their noisome atmosphere. In Covent Garden a filthy and noisy market was held close to the dwellings of the great. Fruit women screamed, carters fought, cabbage stalks and rotten apples accumulated in heaps at the thresholds of the Countess of Berkshire and of the Bishop of Durham."

Well, you will say, all this proves what a vast improvement we have achieved. Yes ; but we must remember that Macaulay was writing on that side of the question. Are we not more self-indulgent, more fond of our flowers, villas, carriages, etc., than we need be ; less hard working and industrious ; more desirous of getting the means of indulgence by some short and ready way—by speculation, gambling, and shady, if not dishonest dealing—than our fathers were. I need not follow at further length Macaulay's description of these earlier times—of the black rivulets roaring down Ludgate Hill, filled with the animal and vegetable filth from the stalls of butchers and greengrocers, profusely thrown to right and left upon the foot-passengers upon the narrow pavements ; the garret windows opened and pails emptied upon the heads below ; thieves prowling about the dark streets at night, amid constant rioting and drunkenness ; the difficulties and discomforts of travelling, when the carriages stuck fast in the quagmires ; the travellers attacked by highwaymen. He narrates how it took Prince George of Denmark, who visited Petworth in wet weather, six hours to go nine miles. Compare this to a journey in a first-class carriage or Pullman car upon the Midland Railway, and think of the luxuries demanded by the traveller on his journey if he is going to travel for more than two or three hours : the dinner, the coffee, the cigar, the newspaper and magazine, etc., etc.

There is a passage in the beginning of *Tom Brown's School Days* in which the author ridicules the quantity of great coats, wrappers, and rugs which a modern schoolboy takes with him, though he is going to travel first class, with foot-warmers. Then, in our houses, what stoves and hot-water pipes and baths do we not require ! How many soaps and powders, rough towels and soft

towels! Sir Charles Napier, I think, said that all an
officer wanted to take with him on a campaign was a
towel, a tooth-brush, and a piece of yellow soap. The
great excuse for the bath is that if it is warm it is
cleansing; if it is cold, it is invigorating; but what shall
we say to Turkish Baths? Surely there is more time
wasted than enough, and, unless as a medical cure, it
may become an idle habit. I have seen private Turkish
Baths in private houses. What are we coming to? We
used to be proud of our ordinary wash-hand basins, and
make fun of the little saucers that we found provided for
our ablutions upon the Continent. At the time of the
great Exhibition of 1851 *Punch* had a picture of two
very grimy Frenchmen regarding with wonder an ordinary
English wash-stand. " *Comment appelle-t'on cette machine
là,*" says one; to which the other replies, "*Je ne sais pas,
mais c'est drôle.*" A great advance has been made in the
furniture of our houses. We fill our rooms, especially
our drawing-rooms or boudoirs, with endless arm-chairs
and sofas of various shapes—all designed to give repose
to the limbs; but I am sure they tend towards lazy
habits, and very often interfere with work. Surely there
has lately risen a custom of overdoing the embellishment
and ornamentation of our houses. We fill our rooms too
full of all sorts of knick-knacks, so much so that we can
hardly move about for fear of upsetting something. " I
have a fire [in my bedroom] all day," writes Carlyle.
"The bed seems to be about eight feet wide. Of my
paces the room measures fifteen from end to end, forty-
five feet long, height and width proportionate, with
ancient, dead-looking portraits of queens, kings,
Straffords and principalities, etc., really the uncomfort-

ablest acme of luxurious comfort that any Diogenes
was set into in these late years." Thoreau's furniture
at Walden consisted of a bed, a table, a desk, three
chairs, a looking-glass three inches in diameter, a pair
of tongs, a kettle, a frying-pan, a wash-bowl, two knives
and forks, three plates, one cup, one spoon, a jug for oil,
a jug for molasses, and a japanned lamp. There were
no ornaments. He writes, " I had three pieces of lime-
stone on my desk, but I was terrified to find that they
required to be dusted daily, and I threw them out of the
window in disgust."

"Our cottage is quite large enough for us, though
very small," wrote Miss Wordsworth, "and we have
made it neat and comfortable within doors ; and it looks
very nice on the outside, for though the roses and honey-
suckle which we have planted against it are only of this
year's growth, yet it is covered all over with green leaves
and scarlet flowers, for we have trained scarlet beans
upon threads, which are not only exceedingly beautiful,
but very useful, as their produce is immense. We have
made a lodging room of the parlour below stairs, which
has a stone floor, therefore we have covered it all over
with matting. We sit in a room above stairs, and we
have one lodging room with two single beds, a sort of
lumber room, and a small, low, unceiled room, which I
have papered with newspapers, and in which we have
put a small bed. Our servant is an old woman of 60
years of age, whom we took partly out of charity." Here
Miss Wordsworth and her brother, the great poet, lived
on the simplest fare and drank cold water, and hence
issued those noble poems which more than any others
teach us the higher life.

"Blush, grandeur, blush; proud courts, withdraw your blaze;
Ye little stars, hide your diminished rays."

"I turned schoolmaster," says Sydney Smith, "to
educate my son, as I could not afford to send him to
school. Mrs. Sydney turned schoolmistress to educate
my girls as I could not afford a governess. I turned
farmer as I could not let my land. A man servant was
too expensive, so I caught up a little garden girl, made
like a milestone, christened her Bunch, put a napkin in
her hand, and made her my butler. The girls taught
her to read, Mrs. Sydney to wait, and I undertook her
morals. Bunch became the best butler in the country.
I had little furniture, so I bought a cartload of deals;
took a carpenter (who came to me for parish relief)
called Jack Robinson, with a face like a full moon, into
my service, established him in a barn, and said, 'Jack,
furnish my house.' You see the result."

Then what shall I say of the luxury of endless daily
papers, leading articles, short paragraphs, reviews, illus-
trated papers,—are not these luxuries? Are they not
inventions for making thought easy, or rather for the
purpose of relieving us from the trouble of thinking
for ourselves. May I also, without raising a religious
controversy, observe that in religious worship we are
prone to relieve ourselves from the trouble of deep
and consecutive thought by surrounding our minds with
a sort of mist of feeling and sentiment; by providing
beautiful music, pictures, and ornaments, and so resting
satisfied in a somewhat indolent feeling of goodness,
and not troubling ourselves with too much effort of
reason. A love of the beautiful undoubtedly tends to
elevate and refine the mind, but the follies of the false

love and the dangers of an inordinate love are numerous
and deadly. It is absurd that a man should either be
or pretend to be absolutely absorbed in the worship of
a dado or a China tea cup so as to care for nothing
else, and to be unable to do anything else but stare
at it with his head on one side. With most people
the whole thing is the mere affectation of affected
people, who, if they were not affected in one way,
would be so in another. Boswell was a very affected
man. He says, " I remember it distressed me to think
of going into another world where Shakespeare's poetry
did not exist ; but a lady relieved me by saying, 'The
first thing you will meet in the other world will be an
elegant copy of Shakespeare's works presented to you.'"
Boswell says he felt much comforted, but I suspect the
lady was laughing at him. I like the "elegant copy"
very much. It is certain that in this world there is a
deal of rough work to be done, and I feel that, attractive
and beautiful as so many things are, too much absorption
of them has a weakening and enervating effect.

I have spoken of the luxuries of the table, of the house,
of travel, and of a love of ease and beautiful surroundings.
There are, however, some people who are very luxurious
without caring much for any of these things. Their
main desire appears to be to live a long time, and to
preserve their youth and beauty to the last. For this
purpose they surround themselves with comfort, they
decline to see or hear of anything which they don't like
for fear it should make their hair grey and their faces
wrinkled, and their whole talk is of ailments and German waters. Swift somewhere or other expresses his
contempt for this sort of person. " A well preserved man
D

is," he says, "a man with no heart and who has done nothing all his life." Old ruins look beautiful by reason of the rain and the wind, the heat of August and the frost of January, and I am sure I have often seen in men—aye, and in women too—far more beauty where the tempests have passed over the face and brow, than where the life has been more sheltered and less interesting.

But I must notice before I conclude this part of my subject one of the principal causes of a fatal indulgence in luxury, and that is a despairing sense of the futility of attempting to do anything worth doing, and of inability to strive against what is going on wrong. This is the meaning of that rather vulgar phrase, "Anything for a quiet life"; and this is the reason why with many people everything and everybody is always a "bore." Here, too, is the secret of that suave, polished, soft-voiced manner so much affected nowadays by highly-educated young men, and that somewhat chilly reserve in which they wrap themselves up. "Pray don't ask us to give an opinion, or show an interest, or discuss any serious view of things."

> "For not to desire or admire, if a man could learn it, were more
>   Than to walk all day, like the Sultan of old, in a garden of spice."

"Let us surround ourselves with every luxury; let us cease to strive or fret; let us be elegant, refined, gentle, harmless, and, above all, undisturbed in mind and body." "We have had enough of motion and of action we." "Surely, surely, slumber is more sweet than toil." "Let us get through life the best way we can, and though there is not much that can delight us, let us achieve as much amelioration of our lot as is possible for us."

These, then, are some of the forms which luxury takes
in the present century, and these are some of the outcomes
of an advanced, and still rapidly advancing, civilization.
These, too, seem to be the invariable accompaniments of
such an advance. A very similar picture of Rome in the
days of Cicero and Cæsar is drawn by Mr. Froude in his
Cæsar. He says: "With such vividness, with such
transparent clearness, the age stands before us of Cato
and Pompey, of Cicero and Julius Cæsar; the more
distinctly because it was an age in so many ways the
counterpart of our own, the blossoming period of the old
civilization. It was an age of material progress and
material civilization; an age of civil liberty and intellectual culture; an age of pamphlets and epigrams, of
salons and of dinner parties, of sensational majorities
and electoral corruption. The rich were extravagant,
for life had ceased to have practical interest, except for
its material pleasures ; the occupation of the higher
classes was to obtain money without labour, and to
spend it in idle enjoyment. Patriotism survived on the
lips, but patriotism meant the ascendancy of the party
which would maintain the existing order of things, or
would overthrow it for a more equal distribution of the
good things, which alone were valued. Religion, once
the foundation of the laws and rule of personal conduct,
had subsided into opinion. The educated, in their
. hearts, disbelieved it. Temples were still built with increasing splendour ; the established forms were scrupu-
lously observed. Public men spoke conventionally of
Providence, that they might throw on their opponents
the odium of impiety ; but of genuine belief that life had
any serious meaning, there was none remaining beyond

the circle of the silent, patient, ignorant multitude. The whole spiritual atmosphere was saturated with cant —cant moral; cant political, cant religious; an affectation of high principle which had ceased to touch the conduct and flowed on in an increasing volume of insincere and unreal speech. The truest thinkers were those who, like Lucretius, spoke frankly out their real convictions, declared that Providence was a dream, and that man and the world he lived in were material phenomena, generated by natural forces out of cosmic atoms, and into atoms to be again resolved."

Next I am going, as I promised, to consider those indulgences which become luxuries by excessive use, and in this I shall be led also to consider the effects of luxury. It has become a very trite saying that riches do not bring happiness; and certainly luxury, which riches can command, does not bring content, which is the greatest of all pleasures. On the contrary, the moment the body or mind is over-indulged in any way, it immediately demands more of the same indulgence, and even in stronger doses. Who does not know that too much wine makes one desire more? Who, after reading a novel, does not feel a longing for another?

The rich and poor dog, as we all know, meet and discourse of these things in Burns's poem—

> " Frae morn to e'en it's naught but toiling
> At baking, roasting, frying, boiling,
> An', tho' the gentry first are stechin,
> Yet e'en the hall folk fill their pechan
> With sauce, ragouts, and sic like trashtrie,
> That's little short of downright wastrie. .
> An' what poor cot-folk pit their painch in
> I own it's past my comprehension."

To which Luath replies—

" They're maistly wonderful contented."

Cæsar afterwards describes the weariness and ennui which pursue the luxurious—

" But human bodies are sic fools,
For all their colleges and schools,
That, when nae real ills perplex 'em,
They make enow themselves to vex 'em.
They loiter, lounging lank and lazy,
Though nothing ails them, yet uneasy.
Their days insipid, dull, and tasteless ;
Their nights unquiet, lang, and restless,
An' e'en their sports, their balls and races,
Their gallopin' through public places,
There's sic parade, sic pomp, an' art,
The joy can scarcely reach the heart."

After this description the two friends

" Rejoiced they were not men, but dogs."

An Italian wit has defined man to be "an animal which troubles himself with things which don't concern him "; and, when one thinks of the indefatigable way in which people pursue pleasure, all the while deriving no pleasure from it, one is filled with amazement. "Life would be very tolerable if it were not for its pleasures," said Sir Cornewall Lewis, and I am satisfied that half the weariness of life comes from the vain attempts which are made to satisfy a jaded appetite.

There are many things which are not luxuries *per se,* but become so if indulged in to excess. Take, for instance, smoking and drinking. One pipe a day and one glass of wine a day are not luxuries, but a great many a day are luxuries. So lying in bed five minutes after you wake is not a luxury, but so lying for an hour is. The man who is fond precociously of stirring may be a spoon, but the man who lies in bed half the day is something worse. Then it must be remembered that a single indulgence in one luxury produces scarcely any effect on the mind or body, but a habit of indulging in that luxury has a great effect.

> "The sins which practice burns into the blood,
> And not the one dark hour which brings remorse
> Will brand us after of whose fold we be."

I am surely right in noticing that the rich man is said to have fared sumptuously *every* day, as though faring sumptuously might have no significance, but the constantly faring sumptuously was what had degraded and debased the man below the level of the beggar at his gate. I feel that to be luxurious occasionally is no bad thing, if we can keep our self-control, and return constantly to simple habits. There is something very natural in the prayer which a little child was overheard to make—" God, make me a good little girl, but "—after a pause—" naughty sometimes." It is the habit of being naughty which is pernicious. Can anyone doubt that the man who, on the whole, leads a hardy and not over-indulgent life will be more capable of performing any duty which may devolve upon him than a man who " had but fed on the roses and lain in the lilies of life."

Sydney Smith, in his sketches of Moral Philosophy, notices that habits of indulgence grow on us so much that we go through the act of indulgence without noticing it or feeling the pleasure of it; yet, if some accident occurs to rob us of our accustomed pleasure, we feel the want of it most keenly. Speaking ·of Hobbes, the philosopher, he says that he had twelve pipes of tobacco laid by him every night before he began to write. Without this luxury "he could have done nothing; all his speculations would have been at an end, and without his twelve pipes he might have been a friend to devotion or to freedom, which in the customary tenour of his thoughts he certainly was not."

In Fielding's *Life of Jonathan Wild* Mr. Wild plays at cards with the Count. "Such was the power of habit over the minds of these illustrious persons that Mr. Wild could not keep his hands out of the Count's pockets though he knew they were empty, nor could the Count abstain from palming a card though he was well aware Mr. Wild had no money to pay him."

If we are curious to know who is the most degraded and most wretched of human beings, look for the man who has practised a vice so long that he curses it and clings to it. Say everything for vice which you can say, magnify any pleasure as much as you please; but don't believe you can keep it, don't believe you have any secret for sending on quicker the sluggish blood and for refreshing the faded nerve.

There is no doubt that habits of luxury produce discontent, the more we have the more we want. The sin of covetousness is not (curiously enough) the sin of the poor, but of the rich. It is the rich man who covets Naboth's vineyard. I knew an old lady who had a beautiful house facing Hyde Park, and lived by herself with a companion, and certainly had room enough and to spare. Her house was one of a row, and the next house being an end house projected, so that all the front rooms were about a foot longer than those of the old lady. " Ah," she used to sigh, " he's a dear good man, the old colonel, but I should like to have his house—please God to take him !" This showed a submission to the will of Providence, and a desire for the everlasting welfare of her neighbour which was truly edifying ; but covetousness was at the root of it, and a longing to indulge herself.

The effect of habits of luxury upon the brute creation is easily seen. How dreadfully the harmless necessary cat deteriorates when it is over-fed and over-warmed. It may, for all I know, become more humane, but it becomes absolutely unfit to get its own living. What is more despicable than a lady's lap-dog, grown fat and good for nothing, and only able to eat macaroons ! Even worms, according to Darwin, when constantly fed on delicacies, become indolent and lose all their cunning.

I will note next that habits of self-indulgence render us careless of the misfortunes of others. Nero was fiddling when Rome was burning. And upon the other hand privations make us regardful of others. In Bulwer's *Parisians* two luxurious bachelors in the siege of Paris, one of whom has just missed his favourite dog, sit down to a meagre repast, on what might be fowl or rabbit; and the master of the lost dog, after finishing his meal, says with a sigh, " Ah, poor Dido, how she would have enjoyed those bones !". Probably she would have done so, in case they had not been her own. Of course we all know Goldsmith's *Deserted Village*, and that it is all about luxury. It is, however, very poetical poetry (if I may say so), and I don't know that it gives much assist-ance to a sober, prosaic view of the subject like the

present. "O Luxury, thou curst by heaven's decree,"
sounds very grand ; but I have not the least idea what it
means. The pictures drawn in the poem of simple rural
pleasures, and of gaudy city delights, are very pleasing ;
and the moral drawn from it all, viz., that nations sunk
in luxury are hastening to decay, may be true enough ;
but what strikes one most is that, if Goldsmith thought
that England was hastening to decay when he wrote,
what would he think if he were alive now.

Well then, if the pleasures of luxury bring nothing
but pain and trouble in the pursuit of them, to what
end do they lead.

> "Behold what blessings wealth to life can lend,
> And see what comfort it affords our end.
> In the worst inn's worst room, with mat half hung,
> The floors of plaister, and the walls of dung;
> On once a flock-bed, but repaired with straw,
> With tape-ty'd curtains never meant to draw ;
> The George and Garter dangling from that bed,
> Where tawdry yellow strove with dirty red ;—
> Great Villers lies—alas, how changed from him,
> That life of pleasure and that soul of whim.
> Gallant and gay in Clieveden's proud alcove,
> The bower of wanton Shrewsbury and love ;
> No wit to flatter, left of all his store ;
> No fool to laugh at, which he valued more ;
> There victor of his health, of fortune, friends,
> And fame ; this lord of useless thousands ends."

If these be the effects of luxuries, why is it that
we continue to strive to increase them with all our
might. I have already insisted that I am not speaking of such things as are beneficial to body and soul,
but such as are detrimental. But it will be said, you

are spending money, and to gratify your longings labourers
of different sorts have been employed, and the wealth of
the world is thereby increased. But we must consider
the loss to the man who is indulging himself, and therefore the loss to the community; and further, that his
money might have gone in producing something necessary, and not noxious, something in its turn reproductive.
In Boswell's *Life of Johnson* is this passage, " Johnson
as usual defended luxury. You cannot spend money in
luxury without doing good to the poor. Nay, you do
more good to them by spending it in luxury; you make
them exert industry, whereas by giving it you keep them
idle. I own indeed there may be more virtue in giving
it immediately in charity, than in spending it in luxury."
He was then asked if this was not Mandeville's doctrine
of "private vices are public benefits." Of course this did
not suit him, and he demolished it. He said, " Mandeville puts the case of a man who gets drunk at an ale-
house, and says it is a public benefit, because so much
money is got by it to the public. But it must be con-
sidered that all the good gained by this through the
gradation of alehouse-keeper, brewer, maltster, and
farmer, is overbalanced by the evil caused to the man
and his family by his getting drunk."

Perhaps you will say, what is a man to do with his
money, if he may not spend it in luxury. If, as Dr.
Johnson says, and as we all of us find out occasionally,
it is worse spent if given in charity, are we to hoard it.
No, surely this is more contemptible still. " What is the
use of all your money," said one distinguished barrister
to another, "you can't live many more years, and you
can't take it with you when you go. Besides, if

you could, it would all melt where you're going."
This hoarding of wealth, this craving for it, is only
another form of luxury, the luxury of growing rich. Some
like to be thought rich, and called rich, and treated with
a fawning respect on account of their riches ; others love
to hide their riches, but to hug their money in secret, and
seem to enjoy the prospect of dying rich. I was engaged
in a singular case some time ago, in which an old lady
who had starved herself to death, and lived in the greatest
squalor, had secreted £250 in a stocking under the
mattress of her bed. It was stolen by one nephew, who
was sued for it by another, and all the money went in
law expenses. If then we are not to spend our money
upon luxuries, and if we are not to hoard it, what are we
to do with it if we have more than we can lay out in
what is useful. I have not time (nor is the question a
part of my subject) to discuss what should be done with
the money hitherto spent in idle luxury. We know,
however, that we have the poor always with us, and that
we can always learn the luxury of doing good. In one
way or another we ought to see that our superfluous
wealth should drain from the high lands into the valleys ;
not indeed to make the poor luxurious, but to provide
them with comfort, to give them health, strength, and
enjoyment. I think then that if we are wise men, seeing
that we are placed in a world of care, trouble, and hard
work, from which no man can escape ; and seeing that,
upon the other hand, we are living in a country and in
an age when we are surrounded with all that makes life
pleasant and enjoyable, we shall endeavour to find out
some mode of harmonizing these different chords. It
need hardly be said how far removed luxury is from the

spirit of Christianity, and from the life of its Founder
yet it may reverently be remembered that on more thar
one occasion He showed His tender regard for the weak
ness of human nature by stamping with His approval thι
pleasures of convivial festivity.

What then is the remedy against luxury? I would sa;
shortly,—in work. A busy man has no time for luxury
and there is no reason why every man should not havι
enough to do, if he will only do it. And I am sure thι
same rule applies to the ladies, although a very busy maι
once wrote of his wife—

> " In work, work, work, in work alway
> My every day is past ;
> I very slowly make the coin—
> She spends it very fast."

But speaking seriously, I am sure that in some sort c
work lies the antidote to luxury. When Orpheus saileι
past the beautiful islands "lying in dark purple sphere
of sea," and heard the songs of the idle and luxuriou
syrens floating languidly over the waters, he drowneι
their singing in a pæan to the gods. Religion ofteι
affords a great incentive to work for the good of others
and, in working for others, we have neither the time, no
the inclination, to be over indulgent of ourselves. Sc
the desire to obtain fame and renown has often produceι
men of the austere and non-indulgent type, as the Duk
of Wellington and many others :—

> " Fame is the spur which the clear spirit doth raise,
> That last infirmity of noble mind, '
> To scorn delights and live laborious days."

Nay, even the desire to obtain riches, and the strife afte

them, will leave a man little room for luxury. To be honest, to be brave, to be kind and generous, to seek to know what is right, and to do it; to be loving and tender to others, and to care little for our comfort and ease, and even for our very lives, is perhaps to be somewhat old-fashioned and behind the age; but these are, after all, the things which distinguish us from the brute beasts which perish, and which justify our aspirations towards eternity.

A STORY.

THE READING PARTY.

CHAPTER I.—THE COACH.

CHARLES PORKINGTON, M.A., sometime fellow of St. Swithin, was born of humble parents. He was educated, with a due regard for economy, in the mathematics by his father, and in the prevailing theology of the district by his mother. The village schoolmaster had also assisted in the completion of his education by teaching him a little bad Latin. He was ultimately sent to college, his parents inferring that he would make a success of the study of books, because he had always shown a singular inaptitude for anything else. At college he had read hard. The common sights and sounds of University life had been unheeded by him. They passed before his eyes, and they entered into his ears, but his mind refused to receive any impression from them. After taking a high degree, and being elected a fellow, he had written a novel of a strongly melodramatic cast, describing college life, and showing such an intimate acquaintance with the obscurer parts of it, that a great many ladies declared that "they always thought so;—it was just as they supposed." The novel, however, did not meet with much success, and he then turned to the more lucrative but far less noble occupation of "coaching." He could not be said to be absolutely unintellectual. As he had not profited by the experience of life, so he had not been contaminated by it. He was moral, chiefly in a negative sense, and was not inclined to irreligion. The faith of his parents sat, perhaps, uncomfortably upon him ; and he had not sufficient strength of mind to adopt a new pattern. He was in short an amiable mathematician, and a feeble classic ; and I think that is all that could be said of him with any certainty. There seemed to be an absence of character which might be called character-istic, and a feebleness of will so absolute as to disarm contempt.

A portion of Porkington's hard earned gains was trans-mitted regularly to his two aged parents, while he him-self, partly from habit and partly from indifference, lived as frugally as possible.

" Bless me ! " cried Mrs. Porkington, within six months of her marriage, " To think that you should have squandered such large sums of money upon people who seem to have got on very well without them."

" My dear," replied he, " they are very poor, and in want of many comforts."

" Of course I am sorry they cannot have them now," retorted she, " and it is therefore a pity they ever should have had them."

Porkington sighed slightly, but had already learned not to contend, if he could remember not to do so. Mrs. Porkington was of large stature and majestic carriage ; and had moreover a voice sufficiently powerful to keep order in an Irish brigade, or to command a vessel in a storm without the assistance of a trumpet.

Mr. Porkington, on the other hand, was a little, dry, pale, plain man, with an abstracted and nervous manner, and a voice that had never grown up so as to match even the little body from which it came, but was a sort of cracked treble whisper. Moreover, when Mrs. Porkington wished to speak her mind to her husband, she would recline upon a sofa in an impressive manner, and fix her eyes upon the ceiling. Mr. Porkington, on these occasions, would sit on the very edge of the most uncomfortable chair, his toes turned out, his hands embracing his knees, and his eyes tracing the patterns upon the carpet, as though with a view of studying some abstruse theory of curves. On which side the victory lay under these circumstances it is easy to guess.

Mrs. Porkington felt the advantage of her position and followed it up.

"I never, my dear, mention any subject to you, but you immediately fling your parents at me."

Mr. Porkington would as soon have thought of throwing St. Paul's Cathedral.

After a honeymoon spent in the Lake district the happy pair went to pay a visit to the parents of the bridegroom, and Porkington had so brightened and revived during his stay there, and had expressed himself so happy in their society, that Mrs. Porkington could not forgive him. In the company of his wife's father, on the contrary, he relapsed into a state bordering upon coma; and no wonder, for that worthy retired tallow merchant was a perfect specimen of ponderous pomposity, and had absolutely nothing in common with the shy scholar who had become his son-in-law. Mr. Candlish had lost the great part of the money he had made by tallow, and by consequence had nothing to give his daughter ; but she behaved herself as a woman should whose father might at one time have given her ten thousand pounds. " My papa, my dear, was worth at least £40,000 when he retired," was the form in which Mrs. Porkington flung her surviving parent at the head of her husband, and crushed him flat with the missile. To the world at large she spoke of her father as " being at present a gentleman of moderate means." Now, as a gentleman of moderate means cannot be expected to provide for a sister of no means at all ; and as Mrs. Porkington, not having been blessed with children by her marriage, required a companion, her aunt tacked herself on to Mr. Porkington's establishment, and became a permanent and substantial fixture. Fat, ugly, and spiteful when she dared, she became a thorn in the side of the poor tutor, and supported on all occasions the whims and squabbles of her niece. Whenever the " coach " evinced any tendency to travel too fast, Mrs. Porkington put the " drag " on, and the vehicle stopped.

Mr. and Mrs. Porkington had now been married three years ; and, as the long vacation was at hand, it became necessary to arrange their plans for a " Reading Party."

"If I might be allowed to suggest," said Mrs. Porkington, reclining on her sofa, with her eyes fixed upon the ceiling, " I think a continental reading party would be the most beneficial to the young men. The air of the continent, I have always found (Mrs. Porkington had crossed the channel upon one occasion) is very invigorating ; and, though I know you don't speak French, my dear, yet you should avail yourself of every opportunity of acquiring it."

E

." But, my love," he replied, "we must consider. Many parents have an objection to the expense, and—"

"Oh, of course !" she interrupted, "if ever I venture, which I seldom do, to propose anything, there are fifty objections raised at once. Pray, may I ask to what uncomfortable quarter of the globe you propose to take me ? Perhaps to the Gold Coast—or some other deadly spot—quite likely ! "

" Well, my love," said the Coach, " I thought of the Lakes."

" Thought of the Lakes !" slowly repeated his wife. "Since I have had the honour of being allied with you in marriage, I believe you have never thought of anything else ! "

There was some truth in this, and the tutor felt it. " Then, my dear," said he mildly, " I really do not know where we should go."

Thereupon his wife ran through the names of several likely places, to each of which she stated some clear and decided objection. Ultimately she mentioned Babbicombe as being a place she might be induced to regard with favour; the truth being that she had made up her mind from the first not to be taken anywhere else. "Babbicombe by all means let it be," said he, "since you wish it."

"I do not wish it at all," she cried, "as you know quite well, my dear; and it is very hard that you should always try to make it appear that I wish to do a thing, when I have no desire at all upon the subject. Have you noticed, aunt, how invariably Charles endeavours to take an unfair advantage of anything I say, and tries to make out I wish a thing which he has himself proposed ?"

The Drag said she had noticed it very often, and wondered at it very much. She thought it was very unfair indeed, and showed a domineering spirit very far from Christian in her opinion, though, of course, opinions might differ.

Porkington took a turn in his little back garden, and smoked a pipe, which seemed to console him somewhat; and, after a few more skirmishes, the coach, harness, drag, team and all arrived at Babbicombe.

CHAPTER II.—THE TEAM.

LET the man who disapproves of reading parties suggest something better. "Let the lads stop at home," says one. Have you ever tried it? They soon become a bore to themselves and all around them. "Let them go by themselves, then, to some quiet seaside lodging or small farmhouse." Suicide or the d——l. "Let them stop at the University for the Long." The Dons won't let them stop up, unless they are likely to take high degrees; and, even if the Dons would permit it, it would be too oppressively dull for the young men. "At all events, let reading parties be really *reading* parties." Whoever said they should be anything else? For my part I know nothing in this life equal to reading parties. Do Jones and Brown, who are perched upon high stools in the city, ever dream of starting for the Lakes with a ledger each, to enter their accounts and add up the items by the margin of Derwentwater. Do Bagshaw and Tomkins, emerging from their dismal chambers in Pump Court, take their Smith's *Leading Cases*, or their *Archbold*, to Shanklyn or Cowes? Do Sawyer and Allen

study medicine in a villa on the Lake of Geneva? I
take it, it is an invincible sign of the universality of the
classics and mathematics that they will adapt themselves
with equal ease to the dreariest of college rooms or to
the most romantic scenery.

Harry Barton, Richard Glenville, Thomas Thornton,
and I, made up Porkington's Reading Party.

Harry Barton's father was a Manchester cotton spinner
of great wealth. Himself a man of no education, beyond
such knowledge as he had picked up in the course of an
arduous life, the cotton spinner was not oblivious to
those advantages which ought to accrue to a liberal
education; and he resolved that his son, a fine handsome lad, should not fail in life for want of them.
Young Barton had, therefore, in due course been sent
to Eton and Camford with a full purse, a vigorous constitution, a light heart, and a fair amount of cramming.
At Camford he found himself in the midst of his old
Eton chums, and plunged eagerly into all the animated
life and excitement of the University. Boating, cricket,
rackets, billiards, wine parties, betting—these formed
the chief occupation of the two years which he had
already passed at college. Reading, upon some days,
formed an agreeable diversion from the monotony of
the above-named more interesting studies. Porkington,
however, who seldom placed a man wrong, still promised
him a second class. Hearty, generous, a lover of ease
and pleasure, good-natured and easily led, he was a
general favourite; and in some respects deserved to be so.

Richard Glenville was the son of an orthodox low
church parson, a fat vicar and canon, a man who, if he
was not conformed to the world at large, was a mere

reflection of the little world to which he belonged. His son Richard was a quick-sighted youth, clear and vigorous in intellect, not deep but acute. He was high church, because he had lived among the low church party. He was a Tory, because his surroundings were mostly Liberal. He was inclined to be profane, because his father's friends bored him by their solemnity. He was flippant, because they were dull; careless, because they were cautious; and fast, because they were slow. He had an eye for the weak points of things. He delighted in what is called "chaff." He affected to regard all things with indifference, and was tolerant of everything except what he was pleased to denounce as shams. Upon this point he would occasionally become very warm. If his sense of truth and honour were touched, he became goaded into passion; but most things appealed to him from their humorous side. He was tall, fair, and handsome, the features clean cut and the eyes grey. His manners were polished, and he was always well dressed. He was full of high spirits and good temper, and was a most agreeable companion to all to whom his satire did not render him uncomfortable. Strange to say, he stood very high in the favour of Mrs. Porkington, who, had she known what fun he made of her behind her back, would, I think, have sometimes forgotten that he was the nephew of a peer. He studied logic, classics, mathematics, moral philosophy indifferently, because he found that a certain amount of study conduced to a quiet life with the "governor." He proposed ultimately, he said, to be called to the Bar, because that was equivalent to leaving your future career still enveloped in mystery for many years.

I do not know that I have very much to say about
.Thornton. He was a very estimable young man. I
think he was the only one of the party who might say
with a clear conscience that he did some work for his
"coach." He was not short, nor tall, nor good-looking,
nor very rich, nor very poor. He was of plebeian origin.
His father was a grocer. I am sure the young man had
been well brought up at home, and had been well taught
at school; and he was a brave, frank, honest fellow
enough, but there was withal a certain common or
commonplace way with him. He acquitted himself well
at cricket and football; and I have no doubt he will
succeed in life, and be most respectable, but on the
whole very uninteresting.

The present writer is one of the most handsome, most
amiable, and most witty of men ; but if there is one vice
more than another at which his soul revolts, it is the sin
of egotism. Else the world would here have become the
possessor of one of the most eloquent pages in literature.
It is said that artists, who paint their own portraits, make
a mere copy of their image in the looking-glass. For
my part, if I had to draw my own likeness, I would scorn
such paltry devices. The true artist draws from the
imagination. Let any man think for a moment what
manner of man he is. Is he not at once struck with
the fact that he is not as other men are—that he is not
extortionate, nor unjust, and so forth? But, in truth, if I
were to paint my own portrait, I know there are fifty
fools who would think I meant it for themselves ; and
as I cannot tolerate vanity in other people, I will say no
more about it.

So at length here at Babbicombe were the coach,

harness, drag, and team duly arrived, and settled for six weeks or more, in a fine large house, far above the deep blue ocean, and far removed from all the turmoil and bustle of this busy world. Wonderful truly are the happiness and privileges of young men, if they only knew how to enjoy them wisely.

"I think it is somewhat unthoughtful, to say the least of it," said Mrs. Porkington to Glenville, "that Mr. Porkington should have taken a house so very far from the beach. He knows how I adore the sea."

"Perhaps he is jealous of it on that account," said Glenville.

The Drag said she believed he would be jealous of anything. For her part if she were tied to such a man she would give him good cause to be jealous.

Glenville replied in his most polite manner that he was sure she could never be so cruel.

The Drag did not understand him.

"Confound the old aunt," said he, as he sat down to the ·table in the dining-room to his mathematical papers, "why did she not stick to the tallow-chandling, instead of coming here? Don't you think, Barton, our respected governors ought to pay less for our coaching on account of the drag? Of course we really pay something extra on her account; but, generally speaking, you know an irremovable nuisance would diminish the value of an estate, and I think a coach with an irremovable drag ought to fetch less than a coach without encumbrances."

"I daresay you are right," said Barton. "The two women will ruin Porky between them. The quantity of donkey chaises they require is something awful. To be sure the hill is rather steep in hot weather."

"Yes," said Glenville, "they began by trying one chaise between them, ride and tie; but Mrs. Porkington always would ride the first half of the way, and so Miss Candlish only rode the last quarter, until at last the first half grew to such enormous proportions that it caused a difference between the ladies, and Porkington had to allow two donkey chaises. How they do squabble, to be sure, about which of the two it really is who requires the chaise!"

"I can't help thinking Socrates was a fool to want to be killed when he had done nothing to deserve it," said Thornton, with a yawn, as he put down his book.

"Yes," said Glenville, "nowadays a man expects to take his whack first—I mean to hit some man on the head, or stab some woman in the breast, first. Then he professes himself quite ready for the consequences, and poetic justice is satisfied."

"How a man can put the square root of minus three eggs into a basket, and then give five to one person, and half the remainder and the square of the whole, divided by twelve, and so on, I never could understand; but perhaps the answer is wrong, I mean the square root of minus three."

"Oh, if that is your answer, Barton," said Glenville, "you are fairly floored. Take care you don't get an answer of that sort—a facer, I mean—from the 'pretty fisher maiden.'"

"Don't chaff, Glenville," cried Barton; "you are always talking some folly or other."

"Well, well, let us have some beer and a pipe.

'He, who would shine and petrify his tutor,
Should drink draught Allsopp from its native pewter.'

We shall all go to the dance to-night, I suppose—
Thornton, of course, lured by the two Will-o-the-wisps
in Miss Delamere's black eyes."

"Go, and order the beer, Dick," said Thornton, "and
come back a wiser, if not a sadder man." Dick pro-
cured the beer; and, it being now twelve o'clock at
noon, pipes were lit, and papers and books remained
in abeyance, though not absolutely forgotten. At half-
past twelve Mr. Porkington looked in timidly to see how
work was progressing, to assist in the classics, and to
disentangle the mathematics; but the liberal sciences
were so besmothered with tobacco smoke and so be-
spattered with beer, that the poor little man did not
even dare to come to their assistance; but coughed, and
smiled, and said feebly that he would come again when
the air was a little clearer.

"Upon my word, it is too bad," said Barton. "Many
fellows would not stand it. I declare I won't smoke any
more this morning."

The rest followed the good example. Pipes were ex-
tinguished, and Glenville was deputed to go and tell the
tutor that the room was clear of smoke. They were not
wicked young men, but I don't think their mothers and
sisters were at all aware of that state of life into which
a love of ease and very high spirits had called their
sons and brothers.

CHAPTER III.—THE VISITORS.

BABBICOMBE was full. The lodgings were all taken. There were still bills in the windows of a few of the houses in the narrower streets of the little town announcing that the apartments ' had a "good sea view." The disappointed visitor, however, upon further investigation, would discover that by standing on a chair in the attic it might be possible to obtain a glimpse of the topmasts of the schooners in the harbour, or the furthest circle of the distant ocean. Mr. and Mrs. Delamere, with their two daughters, occupied lodgings facing the sea. Next door but one were our friends, Colonel and Mrs. Bagshaw. Two Irish captains, O'Brien and Kelly, were stopping at the Bull Hotel, in the High Street. On the side of the hill in our row lived the two beautiful Misses Bankes with their parents and the younger olive branches, much snubbed by those who had "come out" into blossom. The visitors' doctor also lived in our row, and a young landscape painter (charming, as they all are) had a room somewhere, but I never could quite make out where it was or how he lived.

"There are your friends the Delameres," cried Glenville to Thornton, as we all lounged down one afternoon, not long after our arrival, to the parade, where the little discordant German band was playing. "Looking for you, too, I think," added he.

"I am sure they are not looking at all," said Thornton.

"Why, not now," said Glenville; "their books have

suddenly become interesting, but I vow I saw Mrs.
Delamere's spyglass turned full upon us a minute ago."
We all four stepped from the parade upon the rocks,
and approached the Delameres' party, who were seated
on rugs and shawls spread upon the huge dry rocks
overlooking the deep, clear water which lapped underneath with a gentle and regular plash and sucking sound.
It was a brilliant day. Not a cloud was in the sky, and
the blue-green seas lay basking in the sunshine. A brisk
but gentle air had begun to crisp the top of the water,
making it sparkle and bubble; and there was just visible
à small silver cord of foam on the coast line of dark
crags. A white sail or a brown, here and there, dotted
about the space of ocean, gleamed in the light of the
noonday sun. Porpoises rolled and gamboled in the
bay, and the round heads of two or three swimmers from
the bathing cove appeared like corks upon the surface of
the water. Half lost in the hazy horizon, a dim fairy
island hung between sky and ocean ; while overhead
flew the milk-white birds, whose presence inland is said
to presage stormy weather.

"What was Miss Delamere reading?"

"Oh, only Hallam's *Constitutional History*."

"Great Heavens !" whispered Glenville to me, "think
of that !"

"Do you like it?" asked Thornton.

"Well, I can't say I do, but I suppose I ought. My
mother wanted me to bring it."

"I think it must be very dull," said Thornton,
"though I have never tried it. I have just finished
Kingsley's *Two Years Ago*. It is awfully good. May
I lend it to you?"

"Oh, I do so like a good novel when I can get it, but I am afraid I mayn't."

"What is that, Flo?" asked her mother. "You know I do not approve of novels, except, of course, Sir Walter's. My daughters, Mr. Thornton, have, I hope, been brought up very differently from most young ladies. I always encourage them to read such works as are likely to tend to the improvement of their understanding and the cultivation of their taste. I always choose their books for them."

"Nonsense, my dear," said Mr. Delamere, "if Mr. Thornton recommends the book, Flo can have it. I know nothing of books, sir, and care less; but if you say it is a good book, that is sufficient."

"Oh, quite so indeed," exclaimed Mrs. Delamere, "if Mr. Thornton recommends the book. My daughter Florence has too much imagination, dear child, and we have to be very careful. May I inquire the name of the work which you recommend?" She called everything a work.

"Oh, only *Two Years Ago*, by Kingsley," said Thornton.

"Ah!" said Mrs. Delamere, "a delightful writer. The Rev. Charles Kingsley was a man whom I unfeignedly admire. Perhaps I might not altogether approve of his writings for young persons, but for those whose minds have been matured by a considerable acquaintance with our literature it is, of course, different. He is a bold and fearless thinker. He is not fettered and tied down by those barriers which impede the speculations of other writers."

"Off she goes!" whispered Glenville to me, "broken

her knees over the first metaphor. She will be plunging wildly in the ditch directly, and never fairly get out of it for about an hour and a half. Let us escape while we can." We rose and left Mrs. Delamere explaining to Thornton how darling Florence and dearest Beatrix were all that a fond and intellectual mother could desire. She was anxious to be thought to be trembling on the verge of atheism, to which position her highly-gifted intelligence quite entitled her; while, at the same time, her strong judgment and moral virtues enabled her to assist in supporting the orthodox faith. The younger Miss Delamere (Beatrix) was doing one of those curious pieces of work in which ladies delight, which appear to be designed for no particular purpose, and which, curiously enough, are always either a little more or less than half finished. I think she very seldom spoke. She was positively crushed by that most superior person, her mother. Flo was gazing abstractedly into the sea, hearing her mother but not listening, while Thornton was seated a foot or two below her, gazing up into her deep-blue eyes, shaded by her large hat and dark hair, as happy and deluded as a lunatic who thinks himself monarch of the world.

The Squire said he would join us. I expect his wife rather bored the old gentleman. We all sauntered up to the little crush of people who were listening (or not listening) to the discordant sounds of the German band. Here we found the whole tribe of Bankes' and the two Irish captains, one standing in front of each beautiful Miss Bankes; and a little further removed from this party were Colonel and Mrs. and Miss Bagshaw, with the doctor's son. Above the cliff, on a slope of grass,

lay the young artist, smoking his pipe and enjoying the
scenery.

"I hope you intend to honour the Assembly Wooms
with your pwesence this evening," drawled Captain
Kelly to the elder Miss Bankes—the dark one with
the single curl hanging down her back. Her sister
wore two light ones, and it puzzled us very much to
account for the difference in number, and even in colour,
for the complexions were the same. Was Glenville justi-
fied in surmising that the art of the contrivance was to
prove that the curls were natural and indigenous, for if
false, he said, surely they would be expected to wear two
or one each.

"My sister and I certainly intend going this evening,"
replied the young lady, "but really I hear they are very
dull affairs."

"They will be so no longer," said he.

"Well, I suppose we must do something in this dreadful little place to keep up our spirits."

"Yes, I must own it is very dull here, and I certainly
should not have come had not a little bird told me at
Mrs. Cameron's dance who was coming here," said the
Captain, with a languishing air.

"I am sure I said nothing about it," said Miss
Bankes, poutingly.

"Beauty attracts like a magnet, Miss Bankes, and you
must not be angry with a poor fellow for what can't be
helped."

"Very well, now you are come, you must be very
good, and keep us all amused."

"I will endeavour to do my best," said the gallant
soldier.

"Bagshaw, come here!" shouted Mrs. Bagshaw right athwart the parade, startling several of the performers in the band, and drawing all eyes towards her. "Bagshaw, behave yourself like a gentleman. Don't leave me, sir; I should be ashamed to let the people see me following that woman. It's disgraceful, mean, and disgusting."

Bagshaw came back, looking ridiculous. He hated to look ridiculous, as who does not? He approached his wife, and said in a low, but angry tone, "You are making a fool of yourself; the people will think you are mad; and they are not far wrong, as I have known to my cost this twenty years."

Porkington, wife, and drag had just passed up the parade.

"I saw you, I tell you I saw you," she went on excitedly. "You were sneaking away from my side—you know you were. Don't laugh at me, Mr. Bagshaw, for I won't have it. I don't care who hears me," she cried in a louder voice, "all the world shall hear how I am treated."

"Look at Miss Bagshaw," said the artist to me. "What a good girl she is! I am so sorry for her!" Pity is kin to love, thought I, as I watched the beautiful girl move swiftly up to her father and mother, and in a moment all three moved quietly away.

"Who's the old girl?" asked Captain O'Brien of Captain Kelly.

"The celebwated Mrs. Bagshaw, wife of Colonel Bagshaw. She was a gweat singer or something not very long ago. Very wich, Tom; chance for you, you know; only daughter, rather a pwetty girl, not much style,

father-in-law and mother-in-law not desiwable, devil of
a wow, wampageous, both of them !"
" How much ? " " Say twenty thou." " Can't be done
at the pwice." " Don't know that—lunatic asylums—go
abroad—that sort of thing—young lady chawming ! "
" Ah ! "
" What do you say to a row in the old four oar ? " said
Harry Barton. " With all my heart," said I. " Let us
make up a party. The Delameres will go, the two young
ladies and Thornton. Don't let's have the mother, she
jaws so confoundedly. Go and ask Mrs. Bagshaw and
her daughter to make things proper."
" All right ! Thornton shall steer; you three; I stroke;
Glenville two ; Hawkstone bow, to look out ahead and
see all safe." And off he went to ask Mrs. Bagshaw,
who was now all smiles and sunshine, and managed very
cleverly to secure the two Misses Delamere and Thornton
without the mamma. And so we all went down to the
harbour, where we found Hawkstone looking out for our
party as usual.

CHAPTER IV.—BOATING.

" MUSCULAR Christianity is very great ! " said the Arch-
angel. " The devil it is ! " said Satan, "see how I will
deal with it ! " In the days of Job he said, " Touch his
bone and his flesh, and he will curse thee to thy face "—

> " But Satan now is wiser than of yore,
> And tempts by making *strong*, not making poor."

Muscular Christianity was at one time the cant phrase.
Can we even now talk of Christian muscularity? For
my part I think an Eton lad or a Camford man is

a sight for gods and fishes. The glory of his neck-tie
is terrible. He saith among the cricket balls, Ha, ha,
and he smelleth the battle afar off, the thud of the oars
and the shouting. I suppose the voice of the people
is the voice of God; but let a thing once become
fashionable and the devil steps in and leads the dance.
When Lady Somebody, or Sir John Nobody, gives away
the prizes at the county athletic sports, amid the ringing
cheers of the surrounding ladies and gentlemen, I suspect the recipient, in nine times out of ten, is little better
than an obtainer of goods by false pretences. When
that ardent youth, Tommy Leapwell, brings home a magnificent silver goblet for the "high jump," what a fuss is
made of it and of him both at home and in the newspapers ; whereas when that exemplary young student,
Mugger, after a term's hard labour, receives as a reward
a volume of Macaulay's *Essays*, in calf, price two and
sixpence, very little is said about the matter; and, at all
events, the dismal circumstance is not mentioned outside
the family circle.

Nelly Crayshaw was talking saucily with Hawkstone as
we came down to the quay. I noticed Barton shaking
hands with her, and whispering a few words as we got
into the boat; and I noticed also a certain sheepish, and
rather sulky look upon Hawkstone's face, as he did so;
and if I was not mistaken, my learned friend Glenville
let something very like an oath escape him as he
shouted : "Barton, Barton, come along; we are all
waiting for you !"

I do not think Nelly could be called a beauty. The
face was too flat, the mouth was too large, and the
colour of the cheeks was too brilliant. Yet she was

very charming. The blue of her eyes underneath dark eyelashes and eyebrows was—well—heavenly. The whole face beamed and glowed through masses of brown hair, which were arranged in a somewhat disorderly manner, and yet with an evident eye to effect. The aspect was frank and good-humoured, though somewhat soft and sensuous ; and the form, though full, was not without elegance, and showed both strength and agility. No one could pass by her without being arrested by her appearance, but we used to quarrel very much as to her claims to be called a "clipper," or a "stunner," or whatever was the word in use among us to express our ideal.

Barton jumped into the boat and away we went, Thornton steering, Mrs. Bagshaw, her daughter, and the Misses Delamere in the stern, Barton stroke, myself three, Glenville two, and Hawkstone bow—a very fine crew, let me tell you, for we all knew how to handle an oar,—especially in smooth water. And so we passed in front of the parade, waving our pocket handkerchiefs in answer to those which fluttered on the shore, and rowing away into the wide sea. Mrs. Bagshaw, who was an excellent musician, and her daughter, who had a lovely voice, sang duets and songs for our amusement ; and, with the aid of the two Misses Delamere, made up some tolerable glees and choruses, in the latter of which we all joined at intervals, to the confusion of the whole effect,—of the singing in point of tune, and of the rowing in point of time.

As we were rounding Horn Point, Thornton said to Mrs. Bagshaw, "Do you know, there are some such splendid ferns grow in a little ravine you can see there on the side of that hill. Do let us land and get some."

"What do you want ferns for?" asked I, innocently.

"Silence in the boat, three," cried Glenville. "What a hard-hearted monster you must be!" he whispered in my ear.

"Oh, do let us land," said Miss Delamere, "I do so want some common bracken"—or whatever it was, for she cared no more than you or I about the ferns—"I want some for my book, and mamma says we really must collect some rare specimens before we go home." Mrs. Bagshaw guessed what sort of flower they would be looking for—heartsease, I suppose, or forget-me-not; but she very good-naturedly agreed to the proposal, and Hawkstone undertook to show us where we could land. We were soon ashore, and Hawkstone said, "You must not be long, gentlemen, if you please, for the wind is rising, and it will come on squally before long; and we have wind and tide against us going back, and a tough job it is often to round the lighthouse hill."

"All right," said Thornton, "how long can you give us?"

"Twenty minutes at the most," said the boatman, "and you will only just have time to mount the cliff and come back."

I heard an indistinct, dull murmur, half of the sea and half of the wind, and, looking far out to sea, could fancy I saw little white sheep on the waves. We left Glenville with Hawkstone talking and smoking. They were really great friends, although in such different ranks in life. Glenville used to rave about him as a true specimen of the old Devon rover. He was a tall, well-proportioned man, with a clear, open face, very ruddy with sun and wind and rough exercise, a very pleasant smile, and grey eyes, rather piercing and deep set. The brow was fine, and the features regular, though massive. The hair and beard were brown and rough-looking, but his manner was gentle, and had that peculiar courtesy which makes many a Devon man a gentleman and many a Devon lass a lady, let them be of ever so humble an origin.

Barton paired off with the younger Miss Delamere, Thornton with the elder. Mrs. Bagshaw and I followed, conversing cheerfully of many things. I found her a very entertaining and agreeable lady, accomplished, frank, and amiable. There was nothing at all peculiar either in her appearance or conversation. While I was talking to her I kept wondering whether her outbreaks of temper were the result of some real or supposed cause of jealousy, or were to be attributed solely to a chronic feeling of irritability against her husband. In the course of our walk together Mrs. Bagshaw said to me—

"Your friend, Mr. Thornton, is evidently very much smitten with Florence Delamere."

"Yes, I think so," I replied, "but I daresay nothing will come of it. Her family would not like it, I suppose ; for, you know, they are of a good family in Norfolk, and Thornton is only the son of a grocer."

"I did not know that," she said, "but I have thought your friend had not quite the manners of the class to which the Delameres clearly belong. Mrs. Delamere is perhaps not anyone in particular, and she certainly talks overmuch upon subjects which probably she does not understand. The young ladies are most agreeable and lady-like, and I think Mr. Thornton has found that out. It is easy to see that objections to any engagement would be of the gravest sort—indeed, I imagine, insurmountable. It is most unfortunate that this should happen when the young man is away from his parents, who might guide him out of the difficulty. I think Mrs. Delamere is aware of the attachment, and is not inclined to favour it. Do you think you could influence your friend in any way? You will do him a great service if you can warn him of his danger; if he does not attend to you, you might tell Mr. Porkington, and consult with him."

I promised to follow her advice as well as I could, for I felt that it was both kindly meant and reasonable, although I felt myself rather too young to be entangled in such matters.

. . . .

"Oh what a lovely fern, such a nice little one too. Do try and dig it up for me," said Florence.

"I will try to do my best," said Thornton; "I have got a knife." And down he went upon his knees, and soon extracted a little brittle bladder, which he handed to the young lady, saying, "I hope it will live. Do you think it will?"

"Oh, yes," she said. "I can keep it here till we go home, and then plant it in my rockery, where they flourish nicely, as it is beautifully sheltered from the sun."

"I wish it were rather a handsomer-looking thing," said the young man, looking rather ruefully at the little specimen.

"I shall prize it for the sake of the giver," she said,

with a slight blush. "But I am afraid you have spoilt your knife."

"Oh, not at all. Do let me dig up some more."

"No, thank you; do not trouble. See what a pretty bank of wild thyme."

"Would you like to sit down upon it? You know it smells all the sweeter for being crushed."

"Well, it does really look most inviting." Florence sat down, saying as she did so, "How lovely the wild flowers are—heather and harebells."

"Let me gather some for you." He began plucking the flowers, which flourished in such profusion and variety that a nosegay grew in every foot of turf. "When do you think of leaving Babbicombe?"

"In two or three days."

"So soon!"

"Yes; for papa has to go back to attend to his Quarter Sessions."

"I am very, very sorry you are going. I had hoped you would stay much longer. These three weeks have flown like three days."

"Why, Mr. Thornton, I declare you are throwing my flowers away as fast as you gather them."

"So I am," he said. "The fact is I hardly know what I am doing." The colour was blazing into his face, and his heart beating wildly. "Florence," he cried, flinging himself upon his knees beside her, "forgive me if I speak rashly or wildly—I don't know how to speak. I don't know what to tell you—but I love you dearly, dearly, with my whole heart. I cannot tell —I hope—I think you may like me. Do not say no, I implore you. If you do not like me to speak so wildly, tell me so ; but don't say you will not love me. Tell me you will love me—if you can."

Florence was young, and was taken by surprise, or perhaps she might have stopped the young gentleman at once ; but after all it is not unpleasant to a pretty girl to see a good-looking young lad at her feet and to listen to his passionate words of homage. At length, when he seemed to come to a pause, she replied : "Oh, Mr. Thornton, please, please do not talk so. This is so sudden. Our parents know nothing of this !"

"Do you love me—tell me ?"

"We are too young. You really must not—"

"It does not matter about being young."

"Oh, do not speak any more."

"Florence, do you love me? I shall go mad if you will not answer." He seized her hand as he leant forward, and gazed eagerly into her face, while he trembled violently with his own emotion. "Do you love me—say ?"

"I think, I think—I do," she said very softly, looking him full in the face, while he seized her round the waist, and her head leant for one moment on his shoulder, and he kissed her forehead.

She started up, saying, "Oh, do let me go, please. I ought not to have said so."

He rose first, and lifted her up by the hand.

. . . .

"I will tell you what it is, Hawkstone," said Glenville. "I think it is a d——d shame, and I shall tell him so. He may be a bigger fellow than I, but I could punch his head for him, if he were in the wrong and I in the right."

"I dare say you could, sir, and thank you, sir, for what you say. I thought you were a brave, kind gentleman when I first saw you, though you do like to have a bit of a joke at me at times."

"Bit of a joke! That's another matter. But I will never joke again, if this goes wrong. But are you quite sure that Nelly is in love with you really, and you with her."

"Why, sir, we have told each other so this hundred times; and I feel as sure she spoke the truth as God knows I did; and sometimes I think I am a fool to doubt her now. But you see, sir, she is flattered by the notice of a grand gentleman. It may be nothing, but, when I talk to her now, she seems weary like. It is not like what it was in the old days before you came, sir. We were to be married, sir, so soon as the gentle folk have left the town, that is about six weeks from to-day; but now I hardly know what to think. I think one thing one day, and another the next. Sometimes I think I am jealous about nothing. Sometimes I think he is a gentleman, and will act as such; and sometimes I think, suppose he should harm her; and then I feel that if he dared to do it I would throttle him." Glenville could see the sailor's fists clenching as he spoke, and he replied, "Hush, Hawkstone, hush! This will all come right. I feel for you very much, but you must not be violent. I believe it is all folly, and Barton will forget all about it in a day or two."

"May be, may be, sir; but will she forget so soon? When a woman gets a thing of this sort into her head it sticks there, sir. There is nothing to drive it out. He will go off among his fine friends in London, or where-ever it is; but she will be alone here in the little dull town, and it is mighty dull in the winter, sir."

"You see, Hawkstone, Barton is a friend of mine; and, though I have only known him a couple of years, I am sure he is a generous, good sort of fellow, and honest and truthful, though a bit thoughtless and careless. I am sure he will see his own folly and bad conduct when it is shown to him. This is a sham love of his. She is a very pretty girl, it is true. You won't mind my saying that?"

"Say away, sir. I look more to what people mean than what they say."

"Well, no doubt, he has been struck by her beauty; but their positions are different, and he has only seen her for a week or two. Besides, he knows that you and she are fond of one another. I believe he is only idle and thoughtless. If I thought for a moment that he was contemplating a blackguardly act, he should be no friend of mine, and I would not only tell him so, but I would give him a good kicking, or look on with pleasure while you did it. But you must be quiet, Hawkstone, at present, for you know nothing, and a quarrel would only do you harm all round."

"It's not so easy to be quiet. The neighbours are beginning to talk, sir, though they don't let me hear what they say. I can see by their looks. What business has he to sit beside her on the quay? He is making a fool of her and of me. I cannot bear it. Sometimes I feel as if I should go mad. I don't know what those poor creatures in the Bible felt when they were possessed by the devil, but I believe he comes right into me when I think of this business." Then he

bent over the boat and covered his face with his arms,
and his great broad back heaved up and down, like a
boat on the sea. Glenville left him alone, and puffed
away vigorously at a cigar he was smoking in order to
quiet his own feelings, which had been more excited
than he liked.

After a few minutes, Hawkstone raised his head as if
from a sleep, and suddenly exclaimed, " Hey, sir ! The
wind and the sea have not been idle while we have been
talking. We must be sharp now. Shout to your friends,
sir. I cannot shout just yet, I think."

Glenville shouted as loud as he was able.

" That won't do, I'm afeard," said Hawkstone, and he
gave a loud halloo, which rang from cliff to cliff, and
brought out a cloud of gulls, sailing round and round for
a while in great commotion, but soon disappearing into
the cliffs again.

We were most of us already descending when we
heard Hawkstone's voice ; the boat was soon ready ;
but where were Thornton and his lady love ? After
waiting a while, Hawkstone shouting more than once, it
was proposed that someone should go in search for
them. Hawkstone was getting very impatient, and
warned us we should have a hard struggle to get
home again.

" It will be a bad job if we cannot get round the
point," cried he, " for then we shall have to land in the
bay, and although there will be no danger if we get off
soon, yet the ladies will get a wetting, and maybe the
boat will be damaged. We shall just get a little water
going out, for the surf is running in strong."

" It is very wonderful," said Mrs. Bagshaw, " how

suddenly the wind rises on this coast, and the waves
answer to the lash like wild colts. The change from
calm to storm is most remarkable."

" Very," thought I to myself, when I called to mind
the sudden changes of temper which I had noticed in
her.

" What can that duffer Thornton be about all this
long time?" asked Barton.

Mrs. Bagshaw and I exchanged glances. "I am not
sure," said she to me, "that I·have not been doing a
very imprudent thing in letting them land."

It was full ten minutes after the arrival of the rest of
the party before Thornton and Florence made their
appearance, looking very confused and awkward. Glenville preceded them, shouting and laughing. " Here
they are, caught at last, and apparently quite pleased
at keeping us all waiting, and quite unable to give any
account of what they have been doing. One little fern
has fallen before their united efforts in the space of half
an hour or more. Hawkstone says he'll be shot if he
lends you his boat to go a row in another time. Don't
you, Hawkstone?"

" No, sir, I didn't say that. If a gentleman and a
lady like to loiter on the hill it's nothing to a poor
boatman how long they stay, leastways wind and weather
permitting, as the packet says."

Hawkstone pushed us off through the surf, and it was
no easy matter, and, I daresay, required some judgment
and presence of mind to seize the right moment between
the breaking of the great waves. With all his skill we
managed to ship a little water, amid the laughing shrieks
of the ladies and the boisterous shouts of "two" and

"three," who got some of the water down their backs. We were soon under weigh, however, and tugging manfully on, occasionally missing a stroke when the boat lurched on a great wave, and making but slow progress. Fortunately we had not far to go before we arrived opposite to the parade, where a small crowd of people was watching our movements with great interest, and the pocket handkerchiefs again fluttered from the land. The signals, however, met with no response from us. Tug as we would, we seemed to make very little way, notwithstanding Hawkstone's "Well rowed, gentlemen, she's moving fast. We shall do it yet."

The waves were now running high, white crested, and with a long, wide sweep in them. We were forced to steer close to the rocks at the point in order to keep as much as possible out of the tide, which was running so strongly a few yards from the land that we never could have made any way against it there. As it was I could see that for many seconds we did not open a single point of rock, and it was all we could do to keep the boat from dropping astern. Just as I was beginning to despair of ever getting back in safety, and was aware that my wind was going, and that both arms and legs were on the point of giving way, a loud shout from Hawkstone alarmed us all. He jumped up, shouting, "Row hard on the bow side, ease off on the stroke," and in a moment (how he got from the bows I shall never know !) we saw him seated behind the stern-board with the tiller in his hand. The boat shot round, shipping a heavy sea, and we were at one moment within a yard of the rock underneath the parade. "Row hard, all !" was soon the cry, and away we shot before wind and tide in the oppo-

site direction to that in which we had been going. Again
we heard Hawkstone's voice, "Steady, keep steady.
There's nothing to fear. We can run her into the bay !"
Nothing to fear ! But there had been. One moment of
delay, and we should have been dashed on the rocks. I
do not know why it was, but the waves now seemed
gigantic. Perhaps excitement or fear made them seem
larger, or perhaps the change in the direction of the
course of the boat had that effect. Certainly they now
seemed to rear their white crests high above us, and to
menace us with their huge forms. The roar of the
breakers upon the beach added to the excitement of the
scene. The ladies sat pale and silent. I believe all
would have gone well, but at the most exigent moment,
when we were riding on the surf which was to land us,
"bow" and "three" missed their strokes and fell into the
bottom of the boat; and, amid great confusion, the boat
swerved round; and, a great wave striking her upon her
broadside, she upset, and rolled the whole party over
and over into about three feet of water. All scrambled
as well as they could to the shore ; but in a moment we
saw with dismay that one of the ladies was floating away
on the retreating wave, and Thornton was plunging after
the helpless form. Meanwhile the party on the parade
had rushed frantically round to the bay, shouting and
screaming as they came.

"Where's the life-buoy?" shouted Captain O'Brien
vaguely.

"Fetch the life-boat !" cried Captain Kelly, in a voice
of command, although there was no one to fetch it, and,
for aught he knew, the nearest was in London. The
two Misses Bankes screamed at intervals like minute

guns. Mr. and Mrs. Delamere and their younger daughter looked on in speechless agony. The young artist, like a sensible fellow, seized up a coil of rope and dragged it towards the sea. The colonel embraced Mrs. Bagshaw before the multitude.

" She will be drowned ! " cried one.

" She is saved ! " cried another.

" He has caught her, thank God ! Well done ! " shrieked a third."

Thornton had reached Florence, and was endeavouring to stagger back with her in his arms ; but the waves were too strong for him, and they both fell, and were lost to sight in an enormous breaker, while everyone held their breath. As the wave dispersed three forms could be seen struggling forwards ; and, amid the wildest cheers and excitement Hawkstone rolled Thornton and his lady love upon the sand, and then threw himself on his back quite out of breath.

Florence neither heard nor saw anything for some time. Captain Kelly suggested water as being the best restorative under the circumstances. Porkington wished he had not forgotten his brandy flask. The doctor's son thought of bleeding, and played with a little pocket-knife in a suggestive fashion. On a sudden Glenville, who always had his wits about him, discovered the Drag seated on a rock in a state of helpless terror, and smelling at a bottle of aromatic vinegar as though her life was in danger. " Lend that to me—quick, Miss Candlish ! " he cried, and seized the bottle. The Drag struggled to keep possession of it, but in vain, and then fainted away. The young lady soon recovered sufficiently under the influence of the smelling bottle to walk home with the assistance of Thornton and Mrs. Delamere. The rest of the party began to separate amid much talking and laughter; for as soon as the danger was passed the whole thing seemed to be a joke; and we had so much to talk of, that we hardly noticed how we got away. But on looking back I observed that the young artist brought up the rear with Miss Bagshaw, and was evidently being most attentive. Hawkstone received everybody's thanks and praise in a simple, good-humoured way, and proceeded to fasten up the boat out of reach of the tide.

CHAPTER V.—THE BALL.

MRS. PORKINGTON, attired in the white silk which we all knew so well, reclined upon the sofa. Porkington, who was, or should be, her lord and master, was perched upon the music stool. The Drag, in a pink muslin of a draggled description, sat in a deep easy chair, displaying a great deal of skinny ancle and large feet.

"It has always surprised me, my dear," said Mrs. Porkington, "how fond you are of dancing."

"Why, what can you mean?" said he. "Why, I never danced in my life."

"Oh, of course not," replied she. "I am aware you cannot dance, nor did I insinuate that you could, my dear, nor did I say so that I am aware. But you enjoy these balls so much, you know you do."

"Well, yes," he said, languidly, "I like to see the young folks enjoy themselves."

"Now, for my part," said his wife, "I am sure I am getting quite tired, and wish the balls were at an end."

·" My dear, I am sure I thought you liked them, or I would never have taken the tickets."

" Now, my dear, my dear, I must beg, I must entreat, that you will not endeavour to lay the expense of those tickets upon my shoulders. I am sure I have never been asked to be taken to one of the balls this season."

When a man tells a lie, it is with some hope, however slight, that he may not be found out; but a woman will lie to the very person whom she knows to be as fully acquainted with the facts as she is herself. Which is the more deadly sin I leave to the Jesuits.

" I am sure," said the Coach, making a desperate effort, " you appeared to enjoy them, for you danced a great many dances."

" Aunt !" exclaimed the lady, " is it true that I always dance every dance?"

" No indeed !" chimed in Miss Candlish, " far from it. No doubt you would get partners for all if you wished."

" And is it true," she continued, " that I wish to go to these ridiculous soirees ? "

" Certainly not, indeed," said the Drag, " nor do I wish to go, I am sure ! "

" In that case I can dispose of your ticket," said he. Unlucky man ! In these cases there is no *via media*. A man should either resist to the death or submit with as good a grace as he can. Half measures are fatal.

" No, my dear, you cannot dispose of that ticket," said his wife, " and I take it as very unkind in you to speak to Aunt in that manner. It is not because she is poor, and dependent upon us, that she is to be sneered at and ill-treated." At this speech the Drag burst into tears, and declared that she always knew that Mr. Porkington hated her; that she might be poor and old and ugly, etc., etc., but she little expected to be called so by him; that she would not go to the ball now, if he implored her on his knees, and so on, and so on.

Now, who could have thought it? All this fuss was occasioned by Mr. P. having meanly backed out of giving Mrs. P. a new dress in which to electrify the fashionable world at Babbicombe. Ah me! Let us hope that in some far distant planet there may be some better world where all unfortunate creatures,— dogs which have had tin kettles tied to their tails,— cockchafers which have been spun upon pins,—poor men who have been over-crawed by wives, aunts, mothers-in-law, and other terrors,—donkeys which have been undeservedly belaboured by costermongers,—and authors who have been meritoriously abused by critics, —rest together in peace in a sort of happy family.

At this point Barton, Glenville, Thornton, and I all entered the room.

"Oh, I am so glad to see the ladies are ready," said Thornton. "This will be our last ball, and we ought to make a happy evening of it. Are you not sorry we are coming to the end of our gaieties, Miss Candlish?"

"Sorry!" exclaimed the Drag, ferociously. "Sorry! I never was more pleased—pleased—pleased!" Every time she repeated the word "pleased" she launched it at the head of the unfortunate tutor, as if she hoped her words would turn into brickbats ere they reached him.

"I am glad to see you are going, however," said Glenville.

"There you are mistaken," said the Aunt, "for Mr.

G

Porkington has been so very kind as to say he had rather I did not go."

"Really, really," cried Porkington, "I can assure you it is quite the reverse. I am so misunderstood that really I am sure I can't tell——"

"Oh, pray do not disappoint us in our last evening together, Miss Candlish," said Glenville, coming to the rescue of the unfortunate tutor, and speaking in his most fascinating manner. "I have hoped for the pleasure of a quadrille and lancers and" (with an effort) "a waltz with you this evening if you will allow me."

The Drag became calm, and after a little while diplomatic relations were fairly established, and away we all went to the Assembly Rooms, Glenville whispering to me and Barton, "I have made up my mind to get rid of that pink muslin to-night or perish in the attempt." I had no opportunity at the moment of asking him what he meant, but I was sure he meant mischief. However, I never gave the matter a second thought, as the business of dancing soon commenced. Captains O'Brien and Kelly were already waltzing with the two Misses Bankes, and whispering delightful nothings into their curls as we entered. The artist was floundering in a persevering manner with pretty Miss Bagshaw, and the doctor was standing in the doorway ruminating hopefully on the probable effects of low dresses and cold draughts. Thornton was soon engrossed in the charms of his lady love, and Barton, Glenville, and I were doing our duty by all the young ladies. The room was well filled, and, though not well lighted nor well appointed, was large and cheerful enough. The German Band performed prodigies ; the row was simply deafening. There were a few seats by the walls for those who did not dance, and there was a room for lemonade, cakes, and bad ices for those who liked them, as well as a small room in which the old fogies could play a rubber of whist.

Mrs. Delamere had pinned Mr. Bankes in a corner, and was enlarging to him upon one of her favourite topics.

"The Church of England," said she, "is undoubtedly in great danger, but why should we regret it? It has become a thing of the past, and so have chivalry and monasteries. The mind of the nineteenth century is marching on to its goal. The intellect of England is asserting itself. I have ever loved the intellect of England, haven't you?"

"Oh, quite so—ah, yes, certainly, of course!" said Mr. Bankes.

"You agree with me," said Mrs. Delamere; "I was sure you would. This is most delightful. I have seldom talked with any true thinker who does not agree with me."

"I am sure," said Mr. Bankes gallantly, "no one would venture to cope with such an accomplished disputant."

"Perhaps not," she said complacently, "but I should not desire to disagree with anyone upon religious subjects. The great desideratum—you see I understand the Latin tongue, Mr. Bankes—the great desideratum is harmony—the harmony of the soul! How are we to arrive at harmony? that is the pressing question."

.   .   .   .

"Bagshaw, you are a low cheat, sir: you are nothing better than a common swindler, sir. I will not play with you any more. Do you call yourself a whist player and make signs to your partner. I should be ashamed to stay in the same room with you."

Several of the dancers hastened into the card-room. Mrs. Bagshaw was standing up flushed and excited, and talking loudly and wildly. She had overset her chair, and flung down her cards upon the table. Seeing Porkington enter, she cried out, "Look to your wife, sir, look to your wife. She received signals across the table. It has nothing to do with the cards. Look at that man who is called my husband—that monster—that bundle of lies and deceit, who has been the ruin of hundreds."

"By heavens, this is too bad!" exclaimed Colonel Bagshaw. "I declare nothing has happened that I know of, except that my wife has forgotten to count honours."

"It is a lie, sir, and you know it. You are trying to ruin a woman before my very eyes. Oh, you man, you brute! Oh, help, help me, help!" and in act to fall she steadied herself by clenching tightly the back of her chair. Her daughter was luckily close to her, "Oh, mamma, mamma," whispered she, "how can you say such things? Come away, come away; you are ill. Do come." She led her out into the hall, and hurriedly adjusting the shawls, went home with her mother.

Porkington showed himself a man. He took Colonel Bagshaw by the hand. "I am very sorry," said he, "that Mrs. Bagshaw should have made some mistake. Some sudden vexation, and I am afraid some indisposition, must be the cause of her excitement. Allow me to take her place and finish the game. I am afraid you will find me a poor performer, Colonel."

"Oh, not at all. Let us begin. I will deal again, and the scoring stands as it did."

Mrs. Porkington during this scene had turned pale and red alternately. Her husband's dignity and presence of mind astonished her. She was so excited as to be almost unable to play her cards, and her lips and eyes betrayed very great emotion. The tutor's cheek showed some trace of colour, and his manner was even graver than usual, but that was all; and his wife felt the presence of a superior force to her own, and was checked into silence. I had always felt sure that there was a reserve of force in the timid nature of our Coach which seemed to peep forth at times and then retire again. It was curious to mark on these rare occasions how the more boisterous self-assertion of Mrs. Porkington seemed for a time to cower before the gentler but finer will. Natures are not changed in a day, but the effect of the singular scene which had been enacted at that time was never effaced, and a gradual and mutual approach was made between husband and wife towards a more cordial and complete sympathy.

The music had not ceased playing during the disturbance, and the dancers, with great presence of mind, quickly returned to their places, and the usual frivolities of the evening continued to the accustomed hour of midnight, when the party began to break up. I could not find Glenville or Barton. Where could they be? Once or twice in the pauses of the dance I had noticed them talking earnestly together, and occasionally with suppressed laughter. "Now, what joke are these fellows up to, I wonder?" However, it was not my business to inquire, though I had a kind of fear that the combination of gunpowder with lucifer matches in a high temperature could hardly be more dangerous than the meeting of Glenville and Barton in a mischievous mood. Before the last dance had commenced they had left the hall, and, as soon as they got outside, they found Miss Candlish's sedan chair in the custody of the two men who usually carried her to and fro when she attended the balls. Two other sedan chairs, several bath chairs and donkey chairs, and a couple of flys were in attendance. Aided by the magical influence of a small "tip," Glenville easily persuaded the men in charge that the dance would not be over for a few minutes, and that they had time to go and get a glass of beer, which, he said, Miss Candlish wished them to have in return for the care and trouble they had several times taken in carrying her home. As soon as they had gone, he and Barton came back into the ball-room; and, as the last dance was coming to an end, and the band was beginning to scramble through "God save the Queen," in a most disloyal manner, he came up to Miss Candlish, and said, "May I have the pleasure of seeing you to your chair, and thanking you for that very delightful dance?"

"My dear Mr. Glenville," said the Drag, "your politeness is quite overpowering. Ah, if all young men were like you, what a very different world it would be."

"You must not flatter me," said Glenville, "for I am very soft hearted, especially where the fair sex is concerned."

"Ah, how I wish I had a son like you!" sighed the Drag.

"And how I wish you were my m—m—mother!" replied that villain Glenville, as he adjusted her cloak,

and led her out to her chair. It was pitchy dark outside (only a couple of candle lanterns to see by), and
the usual confusion upon the breaking up of a large
party was taking place. Miss Candlish stepped into her
chair, and the door was closed. Glenville and Barton
took up the chair, and, going as smoothly as they could
(which was not as smoothly as the usual carriers), they
turned aside from the main stream of the visitors, and
made at once for the harbour. Here they had intended
to deposit the chair, and leave the rest to fate ; but, as
luck would have it, in setting down the chair in the darkness, one side of it projected over a sort of landing-place.
It toppled over and fell sideways with a splash into the
muddy water. Scream upon scream followed rapidly.
"Murder ! thieves ! help !" Shriek after shriek, and at
last a female form, wildly flinging her arms into the air,
could be seen emerging from the half buried chair.
Glenville and Barton had run away before the chair fell,
but, hearing the fall, looked back, and were at first spell-
bound with terror at what had happened. When, however, they saw the Drag emerge, they fairly fled for their
lives by a circuitous way little frequented by night, and
reached home just before the rest of us arrived. There
was some alarm when Miss Candlish did not arrive for
about twenty minutes or half an hour. Glenville and
Barton told Thornton and myself what had happened,
and wanted to know what they should do. Of course,
we advised that they should say and do nothing, but wait
upon the will of the Fates. They were in a great fright,
and when Miss Candlish arrived in charge of two policemen their terror became wild. And yet they both said
afterwards that they could hardly help laughing out loud.

The pink muslin was draggled and besmeared with harbour mud, and torn half out of the gathers. Its owner was in a state of rage, terror, and hysterics. The commotion was fearful. It was very strange she did not seem to have the faintest suspicion of any of our party. She was sure the men were drunk because they carried her so unsteadily. She was positive they meant to rob her or something worse. She saw them as they were running away. They were the very same men who always carried her. She never could bear those men. They looked more like demons than men. She would leave the place next day. She had been disgraced. Everybody hated her, nobody had any pity. She would go to bed. Don't speak to her—go away—go away, do! Brandy and water, certainly not! and so on. Till at last Mrs. Porkington prevailed on her to go to bed. We had all vanished as quickly as we could and smoked a pipe, discussing in low tones the lowering appearance of the skies above us, and the consequences which might ensue upon those inquiries which we foresaw must inevitably take place.

I never quite knew how it was managed, but two policemen came the next morning and actually examined our boots and trousers, and then had a long interview with Mr. Porkington; and finally we, who were waiting in terror in the dining-room, saw the pair of them go out of the front door, touching their hats to Porkington. I thought at the time that he must have bribed them; but afterwards, on thinking it over, I came to the conclusion that there was no evidence of the complicity of our party. Of course, the sedan men did not know what had happened. Porkington stoutly refused to let the policemen come into our study, and told them he should regard them as trespassers if they ventured to go into any other room. The Drag, although she declared she knew the two men, had no desire to bring the matter before the public. Porkington never said a word to any of us upon the subject, though he looked cross and nervous. As soon as the aunt had taken her departure (which she did the next day) he quite recovered his good humour, and, I believe, even chuckled inwardly at the episode. The *Babbicombe Independent* had an amusing paragraph upon the incident, and opined that some drunken sailors from one of the neighbouring ports were the perpetrators of the coarse practical joke; but we found that the general opinion among the visitors was not so wide of the truth. However, as no one cared for the lady it took less than nine days to get rid of the wonder.

CHAPTER VI.—THE SHORE.

" BARTON," said Glenville, " I want to speak to you, old chap. You won't mind me speaking to you, will you ? "

Barton's brow clouded at once. He knew what was coming. " I don't know what you mean," said he.

" Well, I want to talk to you about that girl."

" What right have you to interfere ? That's my business, not yours."

" If you are going to be angry, I'll shut up. But I tell you plainly, it's a beastly shame; and if you dare to do any harm to her I'll kick you out of the place."

" Out of what place ? "

"Why, out of this or any other place I find you in. You've no right to go meeting her as you do."

"And you've no right to speak of her like that. She is as pure as any child in the world, and you ought to know I would do her no harm. You are trying to insult both me and her."

"Well, I'm very glad to hear you say so. But, see what folly it all is. You know you don't intend to marry her. Do you?"

"Why, as to that I don't know. I'm not obliged to tell you what I mean to do."

"No; but you ought to think about what you mean to do. You know she is engaged to be married to Hawkstone."

"Yes; but I don't think she cares for him a bit—only to tease him."

"Do just think what you are doing as a man and a gentleman—I won't say as a Christian, for you tell me you mean nothing bad. But is it manly, is it fair to play these sort of tricks? I must tell you we must give up being chums any longer if this goes on."

"I tell you what, Glenville, I think you are giving yourself mighty fine airs, and all about nothing; but just because you have an uncle who is a lord you think you may preach as much as you like."

"Oh, come now, that's all nonsense!" said Glenville. "If you are determined to shut me up, I've done. *Liberavi animam meam.* I am sorry if I have offended you. I say it's quite time we went to join the other fellows. They want us to go with some of the ladies over the cliffs."

"Thanks, I can't come. I've a lot more work to do,

and—and I've hurt my heel a bit and don't care to go a stiff climb to-day."

Glenville looked at him, and saw a red glow rising in his neck as he turned away his face and sat down to a book on the table, pretending to read, as Glenville left the room.

The sky was dark, and ominous of storm. It had a torn and ragged appearance, as if it had already had a fight with worse weather and was trying to escape. The sea-gulls showed like white breakers upon the dark sky. The waves roared and grumbled, lashing themselves into a fury.as they burst in white, wrathful foam against the black rocks, and then drew back, torn and mangled, to mingle with the crowd of waves rushing on to their doom. The visitors, dressed for squally weather, in waterproofs or rough suits, walked up and down the parade, enjoying the exhilarating breeze, or stood watching with eager excitement the entry of a fishing smack into the harbour. Far away out at sea in the mist of distant spray and rain two or three brigantines or schooners could be dimly descried labouring with the storm;—mysterious and awful sight as it always seems to me. Will she get safe to port? What is her cargo? What her human freight? What are they doing or thinking? What language do they speak? Are there women or children aboard? Who knows? Ah, gentle reader, what do you and I know of each other, and what do we know of even our nearest friends; to what port are they struggling through the mists which envelop them, and who will meet them on the shore?

An hour had not elapsed since Glenville had left Barton before the latter had reached the first promontory of rocks which shut in the little bay of Babbi-

combe, and on turning the corner found, as he had
expected and appointed, the young woman who had
been the subject of their angry conversation. She rose
from a rock on which she had been sitting, and came
to meet him with a frank smile, saying, "Good afternoon,
Mr. Henry." Somehow the slightly coarse intonation
struck him as it had never done before, and the freedom
of.manner which a few hours ago would have delighted
him now sent a chilling sensation to his heart. "Good
afternoon," he replied, and, drawing his arm round her
waist, he kissed her several times, and held her so firmly
that at last she said, "Oh, sir, you'll hurt me. Let me
go!" Then holding him away from her, and looking
him full in the face, she said, "Oh, Mr. Henry, whatever
can be the matter!" "Come and sit down, darling," he
said, "I want to say something to you." He led her to
a seat upon the rocks, and they both sat down. "Darling," he said, "I am afraid I must go away at once and
leave you for ever." "Oh, no, no, no! not that!" she
cried, starting up. In a moment her manner changed
from fear to anger. "I know what it is!" she exclaimed,
"Hawkstone has been rude to you. There now, I will
never forgive him. I will never be friends with him
again—never!"

"No, darling, it is nothing about Hawkstone at all. I
haven't seen him. But come here, you must be quiet
and listen to what I have to say."

She sat down again beside him. Her lips quivered.
Her blue eyes were staring into the cliff in front of her,
but she saw nothing, felt nothing, except that a dreadful
moment had come which she had for some time dimly
expected, but never distinctly foreseen.

"I hardly know how to tell you," he began. "You know I love you very dearly, and if I could—if it was possible, I would ask you to marry me. But I cannot. It is impossible. It would bring misery upon all, upon my father and mother, and upon you. How can I make you understand? My people are rich, all their friends are rich, and all very proud."

The tears were streaming down her face, and she sat motionless.

"But I don't want to know your friends," she said, in a choking voice.

"I know, I know," he said, "and I could be quite happy with you if they were all dead and out of the way, and if the world was different from what it is. But I have thought it all out, and I am sure I ought to go away at once, and never come back again."

There was a long pause, but at last she rose and said, "Mr. Barton, I have felt that something of this sort might happen, but I have never thought it out, as you say you have. I am confused now it has come, just as if I had never feared it beforehand. I was very, very happy, and I would not think of what might come of it. I might have known that a grand gentleman like you would never live with the like of me ; but then I thought I loved you very, very dearly; you seemed so bright, and grand, and tender, that I loved you in spite of all I was afraid of, and I thought if you loved me you might perhaps be——" Here she broke down altogether, and burst into sobs, and seemed as though she would fall. He rose and threw his arms round her, led her back to the rock, called her all the sweet names he could think of, kissed her again and again, and tried to soothe her ;

while she, poor thing, could do nothing but sob, with her
head upon his shoulder.

A loud shout aroused them. They both rose suddenly, and turned their faces towards the place whence
the sound proceeded. Hawkstone was just emerging
from the surf, which was lashing furiously against the
corner of the cliff, round which they had come dry-shod
a short time before. They at once guessed their fate,
and glanced in dismay at one another and then at the
sea, and again at Hawkstone, who rapidly approached
them, drenched through and through, and in a fierce
state of wrath and terror, added to the excitement of
his struggle with the waves.

"What are you doing here?" he cried, and in the
same breath, "Don't answer—don't dare to answer, but
listen. You are caught by the tide. I have sent a boy
back to Babbicombe for help. No help can come by
sea in such a storm. They will bring a basket and ropes
by the cliff. It will be a race between them and the
tide. If all goes well, they will be here in time. If
not, we shall all be drowned."

" Is there no way up the cliff?" said Barton.

" None. The cliff overhangs. There is a place where I
have just come through, but I doubt if I could reach it
again; and I am sure neither of you could stand the
surf. You must wait." He then turned from them, and
sat himself down on a fallen piece of the cliff, and buried
his face in his hands. Nellie sank down on the rock
where she and Barton had been sitting, and he stood by
her, helplessly gazing alternately with a pale face and
bewildered mind at his two companions. Two or three
minutes passed without any motion or sound from the

living occupants of the bay; but the roaring of the sea grew louder and louder, and the terror of it sank into the hearts of all three. At last Hawkstone raised his head, and immediately Barton approached him.

" Forgive me, Hawkstone," he said, " I have done you a great wrong, and I am sorry for it."

" What's the good in saying that? You can't mend the wrong you have done," and his head sank down again between his hands.

There was a pause. Barton felt that what had been said was true and not true. One of the most painful consequences of wrong-doing is that the wrong has a sort of fungus growth about it, and insists upon appearing more wrong than it ever was meant to be.

" Hawkstone," he said at last, " I swear to you, on my honour as a gentleman, I have never dreamed of doing her an injury. I have been very, very foolish; I have come between you and her with my cursed folly. I deserve anything you may say or do to me. I care nothing about the waves; let them come. Take her with you up the cliff, and leave me to drown. It's all I'm fit for. She will forget me soon enough, I feel sure, for I am not worth remembering."

Hawkstone still kept himself bent down, his hands covering his face, and his body swaying to and fro with his strong emotions.

" You talk, you talk," he muttered. " You seem to have ruined her, and me, and yourself too."

" Not ruined her ! " cried Barton, " I have told you, I swear to you. I swear——"

" Yes ! " cried Hawkstone, springing up in a passion and towering above Barton, with his hands tightly clenched and his chest heaving, "Yes! you are too great a coward for that. In one moment I could crush you as I crush the mussels in the harbour with my heel."

Nelly threw herself upon him, "Jack, spare him, spare him. He meant no harm. Not now, not now! The sea, Jack, the sea! Save us, save us!"

The man's strength seemed to leave him, and she seemed to overpower him, as he sank back into his former position, muttering "O God, O God!" At last he said, "Let be, let be—there, there, I've prayed I might not kill you both, and the devil is gone, thank the Lord for it. There, lass, don't fret; I can't abide crying. The sea! the sea! Yes, the sea. I had almost forgotten it. Cheer up a bit—fearful—how it blows—but there's time yet—a few minutes. Keep up, keep up. There's a God above us anyway."

At this moment a shout was heard above them. "There they are at last," cried Hawkstone, and he sent a loud halloo up the cliff, which was immediately responded to by those at the top, though the sound seemed faint and far off. After the lapse of about five minutes, a basket attached to two ropes descended slowly and bumped upon the rocks.

"Now, lass, you get up first. Come, come, give over crying. It's no time for crying now. Be a brave lass or you'll fall out. Sit down and keep tight hold. Shut your eyes, never mind a bump or two, and keep tight hold. Now then!" He lifted her into the basket. She tried to take his hand, but he drew it sharply away.

"Oh, forgive me, forgive me, Jack," she said, "I have been very wicked, but I will try to be good."

"That's right, lass, that's right. God keep you safe.

Hold on," and he gave a shout up the cliff, and the basket began slowly to ascend. The two men gazed at it in silence till it reached the summit, when, with a rapid swirl, it disappeared.

" Thank God, she is safe," said Hawkstone.

" Look, look !" cried Barton, catching hold of Hawkstone in alarm. " Look how fast the waves are coming. They will be on us directly."

" Yes," said Hawkstone, " there will be barely time to get the two of us up unless they make great haste. I don't know why they don't lower at once. Something must have gone wrong with the rope, but they will do their best, that's certain."

They waited in anxiety amounting to horror, as wave after wave, larger and louder, roared at them, and rushed round the rocks on which they were standing. Presently down came the basket, plunging into the retreating wave.

" Now, then, sir, in with you," said Hawkstone.

" No, you go first. I will not go. It is my fault you are here."

" Nonsense, sir, there's no time for talk."

" I will not go without you. Let us both get in together."

" The rope will hardly bear two. Besides, I doubt if there is strength enough above to pull us up. Get in, get in."

Barton still hesitated. " I am afraid to leave you alone. Promise me if I go that you will not——. I can't say what I mean, but if anything happened to you I should be the cause of it."

" For shame, sir, shame. I guess what you mean, but I have not forgotten who made me, though I have been

H

sorely tried. In with you at once." He suddenly lifted Barton up in his arms, and almost threw him into the basket, raising a loud shout, upon which the basket again ascended the cliff more rapidly than on the first occasion. Hawkstone fell upon his knees at the base of the cliff, while the waves roared at him like wild beasts held back from their victim. He was alone with them and with the God in whom his simple faith taught him to trust as being mightier than all the waves. Down came the basket with great rapidity, and Hawkstone had a hard fight before he could drag it out from the waves and get into it. Drenched from head to foot, and cold and trembling with excitement and grief, he again shouted, and the basket once more ascended. He remembered no more. A sudden faintness overcame him, and the first thing he remembered was feeling himself borne along on a kind of extempory litter, and hearing kind voices saying that he was "coming to," and would soon be all right again.

Luckily there was no scandal. It was thought quite natural that Hawkstone should be with Nelly, and Barton was supposed to have been there by accident. Of course, we knew what the real state of the case was, and were glad that Barton had got a good fright; but we kept our own counsel.

CHAPTER VII.—CONCLUSION.

VERY soon after the events recorded in the last chapter, the Reading Party broke up, and it only remains now for the writer of this veracious narrative to disclose any information he may have subsequently obtained as to the fate of his characters. Porkington still holds an honoured position in the University, and still continues to take young men in the summer vacation to such places as Mrs. Porkington considers sufficiently invigorating to her constitution. They grow better friends every year, but the grey mare will always be the better horse. One cause of difference has disappeared. The Drag died very shortly after leaving Babbicombe; not at all, I believe, in consequence of her ducking in the harbour; but, being of a peevish and "worritting" disposition, she had worn herself out in her attempts to make other people's lives a burden to them. I do not know what has become of Harry Barton; but I know that he has never revisited Babbicombe, nor even written to the fair Nelly. I suppose he is helping to manage his father's cotton mill, and will in due course marry the daughter of a wealthy manufacturer. Glenville has become quite a rising barrister, popular in both branches of his profession, and has announced his fixed intention to remain happy and unmarried till his death. Looking into the future, however, with the eye of a prophet, the present writer thinks he can see Glenville walking arm in arm with a tall, graceful lady, attended by two little girls to whom he is laughingly talking—but the dream fades from me, and I wonder will it ever come true. Thornton, of course, married Miss Delamere (how could it be otherwise), but, alas! there are no children, and this unhappy want is hardly compensated by the indefatigable attentions of Mamma Delamere, who is never weary of condoling with that poor, desolate couple, imploring them to resign themselves to the fate which has been assigned to them, and to strengthen their minds by the principles

of true philosophy and the writings of great thinkers;
by which she hopes they may acquire that harmony of
the soul in private life which is so much to be de-
siderated in both politics and religion. Nobody knows
what she means.

Nelly was not forgiven for one whole year. When she
and Hawkstone met, they used only the customary expressions of mere acquaintances; but lovers are known
to make use of signals which are unperceived by the outside world; and, after a year's skirmishing, a peace was
finally concluded, and a happier couple than John Hawkstone and Nelly cannot be found in the whole country,
and I am afraid to say how many of their children are
already tumbling about the boats in the harbour.

The colonel died, and Mrs. Bagshaw lamented his
death most truly, and has nothing but gentleness left
in her nature. Her daughter has married the young
artist, whose pictures of brown-sailed boats and fresh
seas breaking in white foam against the dark rocks have
become quite the rage at the Academy. The minor
characters have disappeared beneath the waves, and
nothing remains to be said except the last word,
" farewell."

A FARRAGO OF VERSES.

MY BOATING SONG.

I.

OH this earth is a mineful of treasure,
  A goblet, that's full to the brim,
And each man may take for his pleasure
  The thing that's most pleasant to him ;
Then let all, who are birds of my feather,
  Throw heart and soul into my song ;
Mark the time, pick it up all together,
  And merrily row it along.

> Hurrah, boys, or losing or winning,
>   Feel your stretchers and make the blades
>   bend ;
> Hard on to it, catch the beginning,
>   And pull it clean through to the end.

II.

I'll admit 'tis delicious to plunge in
  Clear pools, with their shadows at rest ;
'Tis nimble to parry, or lunge in
  Your foil at the enemy's chest ;

'Tis rapture to take a man's wicket,
  Or lash round to leg for a four ;
But somehow the glories of cricket
  Depend on the state of the score.

  But in boating, or losing or winning,
    Though victory may not attend ;
  Oh, 'tis jolly to catch the beginning,
    And pull it clean through to the end.

III.

'Tis brave over hill and dale sweeping,
  To be in at the death of the fox ;
Or to whip, where the salmon are leaping,
  The river that roars o'er the rocks ;
'Tis prime to bring down the cock pheasant ;
  And yachting is certainly great ;
But, beyond all expression, 'tis pleasant
  To row in a rattling good eight.

  Then, hurrah, boys, or losing or winning,
    What matter what labour we spend ?
  Hard on to it, catch the beginning,
    And pull it clean through to the end.

IV.

Shove her off ! Half a stroke ! Now, get ready !
  Five seconds ! Four, three, two, one, gun !
Well started ! Well rowed ! Keep her steady !
  You'll want all your wind e'er you've done.
Now you're straight ! Let the pace become swifter !
  Roll the wash to the left and the right !

Pick it up all together, and lift her,
As though she would bound out of sight !

Hurrah, Hall ! Hall, now you're winning,
Feel your stretchers and make the blades
bend ;
Hard on to it, catch the beginning,
And pull it clean through to the end.

v.

Bump ! Bump ! O ye gods, how I pity
The ears those sweet sounds never heard ;
More tuneful than loveliest ditty
E'er poured from the throat of a bird.
There's a prize for each honest endeavour,
But none for the man who's a shirk ;
And the pluck that we've showed on the river,
Shall tell in the rest of our work.

At the last, whether losing or winning,
This thought with all memories blend,—
We forgot not to catch the beginning,
And we pulled it clean through to the end.

LETTER FROM THE TOWN MOUSE TO THE COUNTRY MOUSE.

I.

OH for a field, my friend ; oh for a field !
  I ask no more
Than one plain field, shut in by hedgerows four,
Contentment sweet to yield.
For I am not fastidious,
  And, with a proud demeanour, I
Will not affect invidious
  Distinctions about scenery.
I sigh not for the fir trees where they rise
Against Italian skies,
    Swiss lakes, or Scottish heather,
    Set off with glorious weather ;
      Such sights as these
      The most exacting please ;
But I, lone wanderer in London streets,
Where every face one meets
        Is full of care,
        And seems to wear
        A troubled air,
        Of being late for some affair
      Of life or death :—thus I, ev'n I,
Long for a field of grass, flat, square, and green
Thick hedges set between,
        Without or house or bield,
        A sense of quietude to yield ;
      And heave my longing sigh,
Oh for a field, my friend ; oh for a field !

II.

For here the loud streets roar themselves to rest
  With hoarseness every night;
  And greet returning light
With noise and roar, renewed with greater zest.
  Where'er I go,
  Full well I know
The eternal grinding wheels will never cease.
There is no place of peace !
  Rumbling, roaring, and rushing,
  Hurrying, crowding, and crushing,
Noise and confusion, and worry, and fret,
From early morning to late sunset—
Ah me ! but when shall I respite get—
What cave can hide me, or what covert shield ?
  So still I sigh,
  And raise my cry,
Oh for a field, my friend ; oh for a field !

III.

Oh for a field, where all concealed,
  From this life's fret and noise,
I sip delights from rural sights,
  And simple rustic joys.
Where, stretching forth my limbs at rest,
  I lie and think what likes me best ;
Or stroll about where'er I list,
  Nor fear to be run over
By sheep, contented to exist
  Only on grass and clover.

In town, as through the throng I steer,
　　Confiding in the Muses,
My finest thoughts are drowned in fear
　　Of cabs and omnibuses.
I dream I'm on Parnassus hill,
　　With laurels whispering o'er me,
When suddenly I feel a chill—
　　What was it passed before me ?
A lady bowed her gracious head
　　From yonder natty brougham—
The windows were as dull as lead,
　　I didn't know her through them.
She'll say I saw her, cut her dead,—
　　I've lost my opportunity ;
I take my hat off when she's fled,
　　And bow to the community !
Or sometimes comes a hansom cab,
　　Just as I near the crossing ;
The "cabby" gives his reins a grab,
　　The steed is wildly tossing.
Me, haply fleeing from his horse,
He greets with language somewhat coarse,
　　To which there's no replying ;
A brewer's dray comes down that way,
　　And simply sends me flying !
I try the quiet streets, but there
I find an all-pervading air
Of death in life, which my despair
　　In no degree diminishes.
Then homewards wend my weary way,
And read dry law books as I may,
No solace will they yield.

And so the sad day finishes
With one long sigh and yearning cry,
Oh for a field, my friend ; oh for a field !

IV.

The fields are bright, and all bedight
  With buttercups and daisies ;
Oh, how I long to quit the throng
  Of human forms and faces :
The vain delights, the empty shows,
  The toil and care bewild'rin',
To feel once more the sweet repose
  Calm Nature gives her children.
At times the thrush shall sing, and hush
  The twitt'ring yellow-hammer ;
The blackbird fluster from the bush
  With panic-stricken clamour ;
The finch in thistles hide from sight,
  And snap the seeds and toss 'em ;
The blue-tit hop, with pert delight,
  About the crab-tree blossom ;.
The homely robin shall draw near,
  And sing a song most tender ;
The black-cap whistle soft and clear,
  Swayed on a twig top slender ;
The weasel from the hedge-row creep,
  So crafty and so cruel,
The rabbit from the tussock leap,
  And splash the frosty jewel.
I care not what the season be—
  Spring, summer, autumn, winter—
In morning sweet, or noon-day heat,

Or when the moonbeams glint, or
When rosy beams and fiery gleams,
And floods of golden yellow,
Proclaim the sweetest hour of all—
The evening mild and mellow.
There, though the spring shall backward keep,
And loud the March winds bluster,
The white anemone shall peep
Through loveliest leaves in cluster.
There primrose pale or violet blue
Shall gleam between the grasses ;
And stitchwort white fling starry light,
And blue bells blaze in masses.
As summer grows and spring-time goes,
O'er all the hedge shall ramble
The woodbine and the wilding rose,
And blossoms of the bramble.
When autumn comes, the leafy ways
To red and yellow turning,
With hips and haws the hedge shall blaze,
And scarlet briony burning.
When winter reigns and sheets of snow,
The flowers and grass lie under ;
The sparkling hoar frost yet shall show,
A world of fairy wonder.
To me more dear such scenes appear,
Than this eternal racket,
No longer will I fret and fag !
Hey ! call a cab, bring down my bag,
And help me quick to pack it.
For here one must go where every one goes,
And meet shoals of people whom one never knows,

Till it makes a poor fellow dyspeptic ;
And the world wags along with its sorrows and shows,
And will do just the same when I'm dead I suppose ;
And I'm rapidly growing a sceptic.
For its oh, alas, well-a-day, and a-lack !
I've a pain in my head and an ache in my back ;
A terrible cold that makes me shiver,
And a general sense of a dried-up liver ;
And I feel I can hardly bear it.
And it's oh for a field with four hedgerows,
And the bliss which comes from an hour's repose,
And a true, true friend to share it.

PROTHALAMION.

The following " Prothalamion" was recently discovered among some other rubbish in Pope's Villa at
Twickenham. It was written on the backs of old
envelopes, and has evidently not received the master's
last touches. Some of the lines afford an admirable
instance of the way in which great authors frequently
repeat themselves.

Nothing so true as what you once let fall,—
" To growl at something is the lot of all ;
Contentment is a gem on earth unknown,
And Perfect Happiness the wizard's stone.
Give me," you cried, " to see my duty clear,
And room to work, unhindered in my sphere ;

To live my life, and work my work alone,
Unloved while living, and unwept when gone.
Let none my triumphs or my failures share,
Nor leave a sorrowing wife and joyful heir."

Go, like St. Simon, on your lonely tower, ,
Wish to make all men good, but want the power.
Freedom you'll have, but still will lack the thrall,—
The bond of sympathy, which binds us all.
Children and wives are hostages to fame,
But aids and helps in every useful aim.

You answer, " Look around, where'er you will,
Experience teaches the same lesson still.
Mark how the world, full nine times out of ten,
To abject drudgery dooms its married men:
A slave at first, before the knot is tied,
But soon a mere appendage to the bride;
A cover, next, to shield her arts from blame;
At home ill-tempered, but abroad quite tame;
In fact, her servant; though, in name, her lord;
Alive, neglected; but, defunct, adored."

This picture, friend, is surely overdone,
You paint the tribe by drawing only one;
Or from one peevish grunt, in haste, conclude
The man's whole life with misery imbued.

Say, what can Horace want to crown his life,
Blest with eight little urchins, and a wife?
His lively grin proclaims the man is blest,
Here perfect happiness must be confessed !

Hark, hear that melancholy shriek, alack !--
That vile lumbago keeps him on the rack.

This evil vexed not Courthope's happy ways,
Who wants no extra coat on coldest days.
His face, his walk, his dress—whate'er you scan,
He stands revealed the prosperous gentleman.
Still must he groan each Sabbath, while he hears
The hoarse Gregorians vex his tortured ears.

Sure Bosanquet true happiness must know,
While wit and wisdom mingle as they flow,
Him Bromley Sunday scholars will obey ;
For him e'en Leech will work a good half day ;
He strives to hide the fear he still must feel,
Lest sharp Jack Frost should catch his Marshal Niel.

Peace to all such ; but were there one, whose fires
True genius kindles and fair fame inspires ;
Blest with demurrers, statements, counts, and pleas,
And born to arbitrations, briefs, and fees ;
Should such a man, couched on his easy throne,
(Unlike the Turk) desire to live alone ;
View every virgin with distrustful eyes,
And dread those arts, which suitors mostly prize,
Alike averse to blame, or to commend,
Not quite their foe, but something less than friend ;
Dreading e'en widows, when by these besieged ;
And so obliging, that he ne'er obliged ;
Who, in all marriage contracts, looks for flaws,
And sits, and meditates on Salic laws ;
While Pall Mall bachelors proclaim his praise,
And spinsters wonder at his works and ways ;

Who would not smile if such a man there be?
Who would not weep if Atticus were he?

Oh, blest beyond the common lot are they,
On whom Contentment sheds her cheerful ray ;
Who find in Duty's path unmixed delight,
And perfect Pleasure in pursuit of Right ;
Thankful for every Joy they feel, or share,
Unsought for blessings, like the light and air,
And grateful even for the ills they bear ;
Wedded or single, taking nought amiss,
And learning that Content is more than Bliss.

Oh, friend, may each domestic joy be thine,
Be no unpleasing melancholy mine.
As rolling years disclose the will of Fate,
I see you wedded to some equal mate ;
Thronged by a crowd of growing girls and boys,
A heap of troubles, but a host of joys.
On sights like these, should length of days attend,
Still may good luck pursue you to the end ;
Still heaven vouchsafe the gifts it has in store ;
Still make you, what you would be, more and more;
Preserve you happy, cheerful, and serene,
Blest with your young retainers, and your Queen.

YOUNG ENGLAND.

THE times still "grow to something strange";
We rap and turn the tables;
We fire our guns at awful range;
We lay Atlantic cables;
We bore the hills, we bridge the seas—
To me 'tis better far
To sit before my fire at ease,
And smoke a mild cigar.

We start gigantic bubble schemes,—
Whoever *can* invent 'em !— .
How splendid the prospectus seems,
With int'rest cent. per centum
His shares the holder, startled, sees
At eighty below par :
I dawdle to my club at ease,
And light a mild cigar.

We pickle peas, we lock up sound,
We bottle electricity;
We run our railways underground,
Our trams above in this city
We fly balloons in calm or breeze,
And tumble from the car;
I wander down Pall Mall at ease,
And smoke a mild cigar.

I

Some strive to get a post or place,
  Or entrée to society;
Or after wealth or pleasure race,
  Or any notoriety;
Or snatch at titles or degrees,
  At ribbon, cross, or star:
I elevate my limbs at ease,
  And smoke a mild cigar.

Some people strive for manhood right
  With riots or orations;
For anti-vaccination fight,
  Or temperance demonstrations:
I gently smile at things like these,
  And, 'mid the clash and jar,
I sit in my arm-chair at ease,
  And smoke a mild cigar.

They say young ladies all demand
  A smart barouche and pair,
Two flunkies at the door to stand,
  A mansion in May Fair:
I can't afford such things as these,
  I hold it safer far
To sip my claret at my ease,
  And smoke a mild cigar

It may be proper one should take
  One's place in the creation;
It may be very right to make
  A choice of some vocation;

With such remarks one quite agrees,
So sensible they are :
I much prefer to take my ease,
And smoke a mild cigar.

They say our morals are so so,
Religion still more hollow ;
And where the upper classes go,
The lower always follow ;
That honour lost with grace and ease
Your fortunes will not mar :
That's not so well ; but, if you please,
We'll light a fresh cigar.

Rank heresy is fresh and green,
E'en womenkind have caught it ;
They say the Bible doesn't mean
What people always thought it ;
That miracles are what you please,
Or nature's order mar :
I read the last review at ease,
And smoke a mild cigar.

Some folks who make a fearful fuss,
In eighteen ninety-seven,
Say, heaven will either come to us,
Or we shall go to heaven ;
They settle it just as they please ;
But, though it mayn't be far,
At any rate there's time with ease
To light a fresh cigar.

It may be there is something true ;
   It may be one might find it ;
It may be, if one looked life through,
   That something lies behind it ;
It may be, p'raps, for aught one sees,
   The things that may be, are :
I'm growing serious—if you please
   We'll light a fresh cigar.

AN OLDE LYRIC.

I.

OH, saw ye my own true love, I praye,
   My own true love so sweete?
For the flowers have lightly toss'd awaye
   The prynte of her faery feete.
Now, how can we telle if she passed us bye?
   Is she darke or fayre to see?
Like sloes are her eyes, or blue as the skies?
   Is't braided her haire or free?

II.

Oh, never by outward looke or signe,
   My true love shall ye knowe ;
There be many as fayre, and many as fyne,
   And many as brighte to showe.
But if ye coude looke with angel's eyes,
   Which into the soule can see,
She then would be seene as the matchless Queene
   Of Love and of Puritie.

LULLABY.

SLEEP, little baby, sleep, love, sleep !
 Evening is coming, and night is nigh ;
Under the lattice the little birds cheep,
 All will be sleeping by and by.
  Sleep, little baby, sleep.

Sleep, little baby, sleep, love, sleep !
 Darkness is creeping along the sky ;
Stars at the casement glimmer and peep,
 Slowly the moon comes sailing by.
  Sleep, little baby, sleep.

Sleep, little baby, sleep, love, sleep !
 Sleep till the dawning has dappled the sky ;
Under the lattice the little birds cheep,
 All will be waking by and by.
  Sleep, little baby, sleep.

ISLE OF WIGHT—SPRING, 1891.

I KNOW not what the cause may be,
 Or whether there be one or many ;
But this year's Spring has seemed to me
 More exquisite than any.

What happy days we spent together
 In that fair Isle of primrose flowers !

How brilliant was the April weather !
What glorious sunshine and what showers !

I think the leaves peeped out and in
    At every change from cold to heat ;
The grass threw off a livelier sheen
    ·From dewdrops sparkling at our feet.

What wealth of early bloom was there—
    The wind flow'r and the primrose pale,
On bank or copse, and orchis rare,
    And cowslip covering Wroxhall dale.

And, oh, the splendour of the sea,—
    The blue belt glimmering soft and far,
Through many a tumbled rock and tree
    Strewn 'neath the overhanging scar !

'Tis twenty years and more, since here,
    As man and wife we sought this Isle,
Dear to us both, O wife most dear,
    And we can greet it with a smile.

Not now alone we come once more,
    But bringing young ones of our brood—
One boy (Salopian), and four
    Girls, blooming into maidenhood.

And I had late begun to fret
    And sicken at the sordid town—
The crime, the guilt, and, loathlier yet,
    The helpless, hopeless sinking down ;

The want, the misery, the woe,
  The stubborn heart which will not turn ;
The tears which will or will not flow ;
  The shame which does or does not burn.

And Winter's frosts had proved unkind,
  With darkest gloom and deadliest cold ;
A time which will be brought to mind,
  And talked of, when our boys are old.

And thus the contrast seemed to wake
  New vigour in the heart and brain ;
Sea, land, and sky conspired to make
  The jaded spirit young again ;

Or hopes for growing girl or boy,
  Or thankfulness for things that be,
Or sweet content in wedded joy,
  Set all the world to harmony.

And so I know not if it be
  That there are causes one or many,
But this year's Spring still seems to me
  More exquisite than any.

LOVE AND LIBERTY.

THE linnet had flown from its cage away,
And flitted and sang in the light of day—
Had flown from the lady who loved it well,
In Liberty's freer air to dwell.
Alas ! poor bird, it was soon to prove,
Sweeter than Liberty is Love.

When night came on it had ceased to sing,
And had hidden its head beneath its wing.
It thought of the warm room left behind,
The shelter from cold and rain and wind ;
It could not sleep, when to sleep it strove—
Liberty needeth the help of Love.

The night owls shrieked as they wheeled along,
Bent upon slaughter, and rapine, and wrong :
There was devilish mirth in their wild halloo,
And the linnet trembled when near they drew ;
'Twas fearful to watch them madly rove,
Drunken with Liberty, left of Love.

When morning broke, a grey old crow
Was pecking some carrion down below ;
A poor little lamb, half-alive, half-dead,
And the crow at each peck turned up its head
With a cunning glance at the linnet above—
What a demon is Liberty left of Love !

Then an eagle hovered far up in the sky,
And the linnet trembled, but could not fly ;
With a swoop to the earth the eagle fell,
And rose up anon with a savage yell.
The birds in the woodlands dared not move.
What a despot is Liberty left of Love !

By and bye there arrived, with chattering loud,
Chaffinch and sparrow and finch, in a cloud ;
Round and around in their fierce attack,
They plucked the feathers from breast and back ;
And the poor little linnet all vainly strove,
Fighting with Liberty left of Love.

" Alas ! " it said, with a cry of pain,
" Carry me back to my cage again ;
There let me dwell in peaceful ease,
Piping whatever songs I please ;
Here, if I stay, my death shall prove,
Liberty dieth left of Love."

TO THE REV. A. A. IN THE COUNTRY FROM HIS FRIEND IN LONDON.

(AFTER HEINE.)

THOU little village curate,
    Come quick, and do not wait ;
We'll sit and talk together,
    So sweetly *tête-a-tête.*

Oh do not fear the railway
  Because it seems so big—
Dost thou not daily trust thee
  Unto thy little gig.

This house is full of painters,
  And half shut up and black ;
But rooms the very snuggest
  Lie hidden at the back.
                Come ! come ! come !

THE CURATE TO HIS SLIPPERS.

TAKE, oh take those boots away,
  That so nearly are outworn ;
And those shoes remove, I pray—
  Pumps that but induce the corn !
But my slippers bring again,
        Bring again ;
Works of love, but worked in vain,
        Worked in vain !

AN ATTEMPT TO REMEMBER THE "GRANDMOTHER'S APOLOGY."

(WITH MANY APOLOGIES TO THE LAUREATE.)

AND Willie, my eldest born, is gone, you say, little
  Anne,
Ruddy and white, and strong on his legs, he looks like
  a man ;

He was only fourscore years, quite young, when he
   died ;
I ought to have gone before, but must wait for time
   and tide.

So Harry's wife has written ; she was always an awful
   fool,
And Charlie was always drunk, which made our
   families cool ;
For Willie was walking with Jenny when the moon
   came up the dale,
And whit, whit, whit, in the bush beside me chirrupt
   the nightingale.

Jenny I know had tripped, and she knew that I knew
   of it well.
She began to slander me.   I knew, but I wouldn't
   tell !
And she to be slandering me, the impertinent, base
   little liar ;
But the tongue is a fire, as you know, my dear, the
   tongue is a fire.

And the parson made it his text last week ; and he said
   likewise,
That a lie which is half a truth is ever the blackest of
   lies ;
That a downright hearty good falsehood doesn't so
   very much matter,
But a lie which is half a truth is worse than one that
   is flatter.

Then Willie and Jenny turned in the sweet moon-
shine,
And he said to me through his tears, " Let your good
name be mine,"
" And what do I care for Jane." She was never over-
wise,
Never the wife for Willie : thank God that I keep my
eyes.

" Marry you, Willie !" said I, and I thought my heart
would break,
" But a man cannot marry his grandmother, so there
must be some mistake."
But he turned and clasped me in his arms, and
answered, " No, love, no !
Seventy years ago, my darling, seventy years ago !"

So Willie and I were wedded, though clearly against
the law,
And the ringers rang with a will, and Willie's gloves
were straw ;
But the first that ever I bear was dead before it was
born—
For Willie I cannot weep, life is flower and thorn.

Pattering over the boards, my Annie, an Annie like
you,
Pattering over the boards, and Charlie and Harry
too ;
Pattering over the boards of our beautiful little cot,
And I'm not exactly certain whether they died or
not.

And yet I know of a truth, there is none of them left
alive,
For Willie went at eighty, and Harry at ninety-five ;
And Charlie at threescore years, aye ! or more than
that I'll be sworn,
And that very remarkable infant that died before it
was born.

So Willie has gone, my beauty, the eldest that bears
the name,
It's a soothing thought—" In a hundred years it'll be
all the same."
" Here's a leg for a babe of a week," says doctor, in
some surprise,
But fetch me my glasses, Annie, I'm thankful I keep
my eyes.

AIR—"Three Fishers went Sailing."

THREE attorneys came sailing down Chancery Lane,
    Down Chancery Lane e'er the courts had sat ;
They thought of the leaders they ought to retain,
    But the Junior Bar, oh, they thought not of that ;
        For serjeants get work and Q.C.'s too,
        And solicitors' sons-in-law frequently do,
            While the Junior Bar is moaning.

Three juniors sat up in Crown Office Row,
    In Crown Office Row e'er the courts had sat,
They saw the solicitors passing below,
    And the briefs that were rolled up so tidy and fat,
        For serjeants get work, etc.

Three briefs were delivered to Jones, Q.C.,
   To Jones, Q.C., e'er the courts had sat;
And the juniors weeping, and wringing their paws,
   Remarked that their business seemed uncommon
      flat;
   For serjeants get work and Q.C.'s too,
   But as for the rest it's a regular "do,"
      And the Junior Bar is moaning.

.

Air—"Give that Wreath to Me"
("Farewell, Manchester").

I.

Give that brief to me,
   Without so much bother;
Never let it be
   Given to another.
Why this coy resistance?
Wherefore keep such distance?
Why hesitate so long to give that brief to me?

II.

Should'st thou ever find
   Any counsel willing
To conduct thy case
   For one pound one shilling;
Scorn such vulgar tricks, love;
One pound three and six, love,
Is the proper thing,—then give that brief to me.

III.

Should thy case turn out
  Hopeless and delusive,
Still I'd rave and shout,
  Using terms abusive.
Truth and sense might perish,
Still thy cause I'd cherish,
Hallow'd by thy gold,—then give that brief to me.

IV.

Should the learned judge
  Sit on me like fury,
Still I'd never budge—
  There's the British Jury!
Should that stay prove rotten,
Bowen, Brett, and Cotton[1]
Would upset them all,—then give that brief to me.

ON CIRCUIT.

Two neighbours, fighting for a yard of land;
Two witnesses, who *lie* on either hand;
Two lawyers, issuing many writs and pleas;
Two clerks, in a dark passage counting fees;
Two counsel, calling one another names;
Two courts, where lawyers play their little games;

[1] Three of the Justices of Appeal.

Two weeks at Leeds, which wear the soul away ;
Two judges getting limper every day ;
Two bailiffs of the court with aspect sour—
So runs the round of life from hour to hour.

AT THE "COCK" TAVERN.

CHAMPAGNE doth not a luncheon make,
    Nor caviare a meal ;
Men gluttonous and rich may take
    These till they make them ill.
If I've potatoes to my chop,
    And after that have cheese,
Angels in Pond & Spiers's shop
    Serve no such luxuries.

IMPROMPTU IN THE ASSIZE COURT, NOTTINGHAM,

On seeing BRET HARTE *come upon the Bench.*

THANKS for an hour of laughing
    In a world that is growing old ;
Thanks for an hour of weeping
    In a world that is growing cold ;
For we who have wept with Dickens,
    And we who have laughed with Boz,
Have renewed the days of our childhood
    With his American Coz.

IMPROMPTU IN THE ASSIZE COURT AT LINCOLN.

Sir W. Bovill was specially retained in an action for damages caused by the overflowing of the banks of the Witham. With great spirit he contended that the river had for three days flowed from the sea.

THE moon in the valley of Ajalon
Stood still at the word of the prophet ;
But since certain " Essays " were written
We don't think so very much of it.
Now, a prophet is raised up among us,
Whose miracles none can gainsay ;
For he spoke, and the great river Witham
Flowed three days, uphill, the wrong way.

PROLOGUE

TO A CHARADE.—" DAMN-AGES."

IN olden time—in great Eliza's age,
When rare Ben Jonson ruled the humorous stage,
No play without its Prologue might appear
To earn applause or ward the critic's sneer ;
And surely now old customs should not sleep
When merry Christmas revelries we keep.
He loves old ways, old faces, and old friends,
Nor to new-fangled fancies condescends ;

K

Besides, we need your kindly hearts to move
Our faults to pardon and our freaks approve,
For this our sport has been in haste begun,
Unpractised actors and impromptu fun ;
So on our own deserts we dare not stand,
But beg the favour that we can't command.
Most flat would fall our " cranks and wanton wiles,'
Reft of your favouring "nods and wreathed smiles,"
As some tame landscape desolately bare
Is charmed by sunshine into seeming fair ;
So, gentle friends, if you your smiles bestow,
That which is tame in us will not seem so.
Our play is a charade.   We split the word,
Each syllable an act, the whole a third ;
My first we show you by a comic play,
Old, but not less the welcome, I dare say.
My second will be brought upon the stage
From lisping childhood down to palsied age.
Last, but not least, our country's joy and pride,
A British Jury will my whole decide ;
But what's the word you'll ask me, what's the word ?
That you must guess, or ask some little bird ;
Guess as you will you'll fail ; for 'tis no doubt
One of those things " no fellow can find out."

TO A SCIENTIFIC FRIEND.

You say 'tis plain that poets feign,
  And from the truth depart;
They write with ease what fibs they please,
  With artifice, not art;
Dearer to you the simply true—
  The fact without the fancy—
Than this false play of colours gay,
  So very vague and chancy.
No doubt 'tis well the truth to tell
  In scientific coteries;
But I'll be bold to say she's cold,
  Excepting to her votaries.
The false disguise of tawdry lies
  May hide sweet Nature's face;
But in her form the blood runs warm,
  As in the human race;
And in the rose the dew-drop glows,
  And, o'er the seas serene,
The sunshine white still breaks in light
  Of yellow, blue, and green.
In thousand rays the fancy plays;
  The feelings rise and bubble;
The mind receives, the heart believes,
  And makes each pleasure double.
Then spare to draw without a flaw,
  Nor all too perfect make her,

Lest Nature wear the dull, cold air
Of some demurest Quaker—
Whose mien austere is void of cheer,
Or sense of sins forgiven,
And her sweet face has lost all grace
Of either earth or heaven.

GLASGOW: PRINTED AT THE UNIVERSITY PRESS BY ROBERT MACLEHOSE.